CRIME IN ITS TIME

TALES OF DECEIT AND MURDER

PAST AND PRESENT

CRIME IN ITS TIME

TALES OF DECEIT AND MURDER

PAST AND PRESENT

MJ Jones

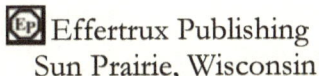 Effertrux Publishing
Sun Prairie, Wisconsin

Effertrux Publishing
P.O. Box 694
Sun Prairie, Wi 53590-9998
www.Effertrux.com

Library of Congress Control Number: 2013952694

ISBN: 978-1-940251-05-9

Cover design by: RL Sather

In memory of Maxine, Pat, Sanford, Tolson

They were the artists.

CONTENTS

THE WITCH AND THE RELIC THIEF

Kingdom of Wessex and All England

Anno Domini 979

"We want you to catch a witch," the abbot said.

"Ain't in the witch business," I said. "Saints are my line."

"So I've heard." He reached for the silver flagon on the table in front of him.

The two of us were drinking ale in the guest parlor of Bracknel monastery. That's down south of London and the abbot's name was Hylltun. He was a little bit of a man, with a doughy face and inky hands that told you he spent too much time on books.

Me, I'm Tryffin ap Tewdwr. I sell saints. Their parts, too, if that's the best I can do—St. Ninnie's foot, say, or St. Peter's sword. In other words, I'm a relic monger. I'm Welsh, too, but even so I've got King Ethelred's warrant to do business with church or monastery, canon or archbishop. Every cleric in England knows Tryff Tewdwr'll find 'em all the holy bones they want. And they're not always too fussy about how I do it, so long as the price is right.

I also do a little bounty hunting. It's not something I'm awful proud of. But saints are scarce in this fallen world and a man has to make a living. Which is why I went to Bracknel Monastery soon as I got the abbot's message.

"Saints're my line," I told him. "Witches cost extra."

Abbot Hylltun pretended like he didn't hear that last part. He went straight to his tale of witchery at Bracknel.

See you, when clerics talk about a witch they mean somebody in league with Satan. I'm not saying I doubt 'em. But the witches I know

1

are mainly old widows trying to scrape by as best they can. They sell charms to the love-struck or the vengeful and sometimes they cure the sick.

You can find a witch's house on the edge of any village in England. Wales and France and Italy, too. Just look for the ailing lined up in her lane. Presently, the old woman'll come out, pass her hands over 'em, mumble a few words, then lay on some herbs. Like as not, the patients walk away feeling much better. Either that or they die. And it wouldn't turn out any different if word and weed came from a priest instead.

At least that's how it is with most witches. But this one, Abbot Hylltun claimed, was a whole other tale.

He took a last pull of drink, then tucked his hands under his black scapular. "For quite a while, we've been finding strange things, wicked things, on one or another of the monastery doorsteps," he said. "Little hearts pierced by feathers, strings of fresh vermin gut, rats with their heads torn off. And blood spattered all over."

Innards and fresh blood on the doorstep sounded bad all right. Like somebody was for sure trying to cast a nasty spell on these monks. I asked who'd want to do such a thing.

"We don't know," the abbot said. "Nor do we know whether it's a witch acting alone or someone employing a witch. But it always happens at night. Therefore, we want you to stand night watch, find this fiend's companion."

For a while, I gazed at the monastery's jeweled ale cups, the silver flagon, the gilded serving dish. Then I said, "Don't misunderstand me, Abbot, it ain't I don't want to help you out. But there's a couple of dozen monks here at Bracknel. How come you don't set a few of 'em to walking the monastery after dark?"

"We have done. On those nights, either nothing happens or it happens but no one sees," he said, blessing himself against this devil's work.

I didn't ask what made him think it'd be any different with me around. Why bother? I didn't mind spending a couple of nights outside, even in February and in the company of a witch. After all, I'd have the monastery's blessing. More important, I'd have the monastery's silver.

But when I named my price, Abbot Hylltun showed he was a true monastery man, close-tonsured and close-fisted, too. Made me bargain harder'n a French fishwife on Friday till I got what I asked. Most of it, anyhow.

Bracknel wasn't one of your Italian monasteries, all neat and square and plumb. Its crooked wood buildings—church, chapter house, dormitory, sheds, stable, brewery—were jumbled up together like timber in an ox cart. Only the latrine and cookhouse, neither of 'em any too tidy, stood by themselves. Around the whole place there rambled a rock wall built high enough to keep the Northmen out and the monks in.

Come nightfall Bracknel got black as the Pit. As I found out when I went on watch by the chapter house door. That's where the abbot said most of the blood and innards had turned up. Right after Compline, I plunked myself in the passage twixt chapter house and brewery, my back against the brewery wall, legs stretched across the narrow alley. That way somebody coming from the south couldn't get past me and, dark though it was, I'd see anybody else.

Just in case I did, I got my knife out. It was a big English scramseaxe and I knew how to put it to good use. Still, even with knife at the ready, I felt a little scared there in that dark alley. Generally, St. Nicholas gives me good protection wherever I am, but evil can creep up on you even in a monastery. And the night'd turned cold. I pulled my cloak tight around me, then took to shivering anyhow.

'Course, I wasn't too scared to get sleepy. That's what happens when you stay up past sunset, so I don't make much apology about it. But if I'da kept full awake, I'da for sure snared the wicked thing that all of a sudden came whipping down that passage. Instead, all I caught was the chill wind of its passing.

I chased after it, you bet I did. Down the alley, up another, across the yard to the cloister gate.

The gate stood wide open. But even with the new-risen moon throwing out some light, I couldn't see a soul beyond. Nor did I hear foot fall or hoof beat. Only thing around was a big black cat, blinking at me from atop the cloister wall.

There was nothing back on the chapter house doorstep, either. Or on any other doorstep in the cloister. Maybe, thought I, the thing in the passage was a dream, some figment of my own Welsh fancy. More likely, it was just a cold wind blowing down an alley. The world's full of unseen spirits and sprites and evil imps, but that doesn't mean they come visiting Tryff Tewdwr.

Still, there'd been a mean feel to whatever blew past me in that alley. The shivers came on me again. I quick-like cured 'em, though, in the brewery.

Whilst I drank the monks' ale, I thought about the wild wind Welsh magicians travel around in. And about how the French claim cats carry evil. 'Specially black cats.

St. Nicholas help me, thought I. What if I've been visited after all? Or worse yet, what if I've been warned?

Next morning, after a well-earned nap out in the stable with my horse, I met up with Abbot Hylltun again. This time it was in the abbot's lodge and there were a couple of other monks with him. The three of 'em sat at a big oak table. On it lay a leather sack bulging nice and fat with what I hoped might be my pay.

"Well, Welshman," the abbot said. "You let the evil one escape you."

He had a black cat draped across his shoulders. I didn't like the look on either one of their faces.

"We'll disregard that failure, however," he said. "Because we now know who our witch is. Not one of your good country grannies, I can assure you, innocently healing the sad and the stricken. We're dealing with a real devil woman. She's committed—"

His voice dropped to a meaningful whisper. "She's committed *invultuacio.*"

All three monks crossed themselves.

First I thought he meant the woman'd been letting the local lads have their way with her. Or, worse, she was having her way with the lads. Then I remembered the Latin the monks beat into me back in Wales.

"*Invultuacio,*" I said. "That's when a witch, with the Devil for helper, makes a likeness of her enemy and sticks pins in it."

"Whereupon the enemy dies a rather nasty death," Abbot Hylltun said.

Just then, the cat leaped off the abbot's shoulder and ran to the lodge door. Abbot Hylltun flicked a forefinger at one of the monks. "Put him out, Cole."

The monk called Cole didn't move and I didn't blame him. He was the monastery's prior—its second-in-command. Abbot Hylltun had no business treating him like a peasant. For a while abbot and prior had 'em a staring match and, believe me, there was blood in their eye.

Finally the third monk—Brother Boda—let the cat out. He was a tall, shambling young redhead with a lopsided, loose-mouthed grin on his round face. Not, thought I, somebody you'd call over-bright. But Abbot Hylltun dropped out of the staring contest to tell me it was Brother Boda who'd found out who had been strewing blood and guts around the monastery.

"While you, Welshman," the abbot said, "were engaged in chasing my cat across the cloister—oh yes, you were seen—the evil one was busy elsewhere. Tell him, Boda."

For a moment Brother Boda looked terrified. Not so much at what he'd found out as at having to put it in words. He grunted a little, groaned some, then gave Prior Cole a pleading glance. "Vuh—bruh—?" he said.

Prior Cole, unlike the bookish little abbot, had the mien of a real man. For one thing he was big. Bigger than me, even. And he had the kind of nose a man gets when he's taken some hard punches. From the size of his fists, I guessed he'd thrown a few, too.

Prior Cole pulled the bulging leather sack across the table and reached inside.

Ah-ha, thought I. I'm going to get paid after all.

He took out a dead hedgehog.

My mouth dropped to my tunic hem, then right down to my shoe tops when I saw it wasn't a hedgehog either.

It was a doll—a doll studded with nails.

Abbot Hylltun took—snatched—the doll from the prior and said, "As you can see, we're dealing with a true devil woman."

"Vuh—dev—vuh," Brother Boda said.

"Take a close look," the abbot said.

At first, I didn't want to touch the doll. You never know what a thing like that might get up to. But after the abbot promised it'd been properly exorcised, I took a deep breath and picked it up.

Except for the nails sticking out of its head, heart, and crotch, it seemed no different from any other little girl's doll baby. It was maybe a foot long, made out of dirty linen and stuffed with straw. For clothes it wore a hooded, full-length black cloak.

"Does kind of look like a monk," I said. "And you say you know who made it?"

The abbot said, "Her name's Aelfreda. She lives nearby."

So, I was willing to bet, did a lot of folk capable of sticking pins in a doll. "What makes you think it came from this Aelfreda?" I asked.

"Dev—vuh," Brother Boda said.

The abbot said, "Aelfreda's work is quite well-known hereabout. Her little figures often turn up on thresholds, in mangers, under doorsteps. They always look exactly like the person they're aimed at and, within a fortnight, that person always comes to grief."

"Sounds like she should've been punished long since."

Prior Cole said, "As a matter of fact, she has been punished. Holy church has several times condemned her to fast on bread and water. Twice it was for three years and once for seven."

Woof, thought I. Seven years on bread and water meant one of Aelfreda's victims had died. She'd have got the same for any homicide.

"The church is a fount of mercy," I said. Then, knowing how hard English law is on witches, I asked how come she hadn't gone before the shire court, too.

Abbot Hylltun took a sudden interest in the tabletop, but the prior's knowing smirk gave me the answer. Aelfreda had friends in high places.

I said, "Any other reason you think it's her? Maybe there's a new witch in the neighborhood. Or maybe somebody wants you to put the blame on Aelfreda."

The little abbot gave me a good hard glare. He said, "That doll is Aelfreda's work, no doubt about it. She likes to stick a nail between the legs."

"Why would she want to plant a doll at your gate? What's she got against you all?"

"Probably nothing," the abbot said. "Our neighbor, Lord Stanfeld, is another matter. And Aelfreda is his churl."

Churl may be the English word for free peasant but all the average churl owns free and clear is his hide. Everything else—house, ox, privy—belongs to the landlord. It's pretty much the same the world over. And it's why tenants pretty much do what their lord wants 'em to.

"Stanfeld," the abbot said, "is a royal thane. As such he assumes that right after Easter, when young King Ethelred gives out gifts at his coronation, he will get King Wood. He's wrong, of course. Bracknel will be the Wood's new owner."

The abbot said King Wood was the forest that lay twixt the monastery and Stanfeld's hall. Until recently it'd been a royal hunting preserve. But twelve-year old King Ethelred, who'd stepped over a dead brother on his way to the throne, would naturally want to make sure the church was on his side. Lord Stanfeld, on the other hand, was just a backwoods nobleman with only the one estate and no son to inherit it anyhow.

Abbot Hylltun said, "We suspect that in order to get King Wood, Stanfeld has laid a curse on us and is using Aelfreda as his cat's paw to carry it out. Unfortunately, we can't accuse him because he is not directly involved. The woman, however, is well known as a witch. She will be punished."

"What you waiting on then?" I said. "Bring her in, send for the king's reeve, and start the trial. Maybe Stanfeld'll get the message. The king will for sure."

Just what he had in mind, Abbot Hylltun said. "But Stanfeld won't let Aelfreda go without a fight. And as all England knows, there are men who have no qualms about visiting physical harm on monks and monasteries. Sometimes considerable harm."

"Quite the lad, is Stanfeld," I said. "Goes in for curses and cudgels both.

"Indeed," Abbot Hylltun said. "Therefore, we can't just have our witch arrested. You must catch her in flagrante delicto." Which meant spending who knew how many more nights out in the cold. But what choice did I have? It was freeze my toes in the cloister alley or limp back home broke as the day I left.

After we went out of the abbot's lodge, Prior Cole said he'd help me catch Aelfreda. He didn't say exactly how. Then, wouldn't you know, Brother Boda up and volunteered, too. The prior sent him to the church-house. "The best way you can help," he said, "is to pray."

It was a good idea, all the way around, and it sure pleased Brother Boda. The grin on the young redhead's face couldn't have been wider. He knelt for a blessing, then trotted off across the cloister yard.

Where the monastery's workday was in full swing. Whilst one gang of monks dug parsnips in the kitchen garden, others were

7

feeding the geese and mucking out the stable yard and unloading a cart full of cowhide. From the far side of the wall came the shouts of somebody chasing down a runaway pig.

We stood beside the forge and watched a little bald fellow pump bellows bigger'n he was. Presently, I said, "I got a couple of problems with this Aelfreda and her dolly."

Prior Cole nudged me away from the forge, to walk along the metalled paths that criss-crossed the cloister. "It's no wonder you have problems," he said. "The abbot, in his splendid wisdom, gave you very little information. How can I make remedy?"

"First off, why'd Aelfreda all of a sudden change from planting blood and guts to planting a doll? And don't say it's 'cause big bad me's around now. It wasn't me that found the doll."

The prior ran a hand over his jaw. "Hmmm," he said, sagely.

"Another problem's got to do with Brother Boda finding the doll. How come he was out of the dormitory, middle of the night? Abbot gave strict orders that from bedtime till the night office, I was the only one s'posed to be up and around."

The prior let out a light laugh. "Oh," he said. "I expect Boda wanted to be the hero in all this. He's not quite the simpleton he appears, you know. He likes to show off. And he's been caught wandering around in the night before. Once he went as far as King Wood, following a tomcat on the prowl or so he claimed."

Poor adventure-hungry lad, thought I. He'd probably been a boy-oblate, walled up in the monastery since he was ten. Chucked there by a father who knew what to do with the family rubbish. Just like mine did. But that's another story.

The prior said, "There's another possibility you should know about." He flicked his eyes back and forth across the cloister. When he saw that nobody was close, he said, "A possibility I suppose I shouldn't mention, perhaps shouldn't even think."

In a low voice he said, "Abbot Hylltun may have wanted to make sure King Ethelred gave the Wood to the monastery. Ethelred's only a boy, you know, and Stanfeld has friends at court. Persuasive friends who know the way to a child's heart."

"So?"

The prior drew a deep breath before he said, "I think it's quite possible that the abbot got hold of one of Aelfreda's dolls—she strews them around like seed. Then he put it before the gate and arranged for Boda to find it."

When I looked doubtful, the prior said, "Hylltun was out of his cell last night. I know because mine is right next door and I heard him leave."

"I didn't see him around the cloister. Hear him, either."

"An abbot can be very stealthy," Prior Cole said. "In or out of his felt night shoes."

That was interesting, maybe even true, but for the next couple of nights nothing more happened at Bracknel. I mean, no evil came our way, though I did catch Brother Boda up and about when he shouldn't have been. Found him sitting on the brewery floor, swilling ale and tossing catmint to the abbot's big black cat, both of 'em drunk as lords.

He begged me not to tell on him and I didn't. Not that night. Or the next, when he was back in the brewery, sober and without the cat, claiming he wanted to help me stop the ev—ev—evil at Bracknel.

It wasn't a bad idea. I could keep my eye on him and he might even turn out to be some use. 'Course, it'd be a hard sell to Abbot Hylltun. But I'd had plenty of experience peddling peculiar things to reluctant clerics.

Brother Boda went on watch the next night and, as the prior'd said, he wasn't stupid. Tongue-tied maybe, but a keen-eyed, silent-footed sentinel—and nobody's fool when it came to monastery politics. As I found out a few nights later when our patrol paths crossed near the chapter house.

"Been thinking," I said to him, "about something around here that seems kind of funny."

"Lot—lot—lot of things funny here. Longer you stay, funnier they get."

"Your prior and your abbot," I said. "They don't like each other much, do they?"

By then we'd opened up our lantern-hoods and I could see Brother Boda pulling at a hank of his red hair. Finally he busted out in a lopsided grin and said, "You really a re—relic thief?"

Ignoring his bad manners, I said, "What is it twixt the two of 'em? Just another clerics' tussle over the power and the glory or is there something special?"

He pulled at his hair some more, before he said, "King Wood. They both want the cred—cred—"

"The credit for convincing King Ethelred to give the Wood to Bracknel?"

He wagged his head up and down. "And for getting Aelfreda caught."

So, thought I, it's politics as usual here at Bracknel. Why ain't I surprised?

"A man who has the king's ear can go far," I said. "At court and in the church, too. Bishop Hylltun, Abbot Cole—names with a real nice ring to 'em."

Brother Boda gave me another of his grins. This time it showed a mouth full of pointy teeth.

Two nights later, whilst I was on watch at the front gate, something hit it with a good, solid thunk. I yanked open the wicket. On the ground below lay a doll. And tearing off into the night went a woman.

When finally I chased her down, I found out the abbot was wrong—Aelfreda wouldn't need Stanfeld and his churls in a fight. She could bite and scratch and yowl worse'n a cat in heat.

Wasn't any need for it, you ask me. All I did was throw an elbow round her neck. A smart somebody would've just stood there till they found out what was going on. But not our witch. She fought. Then when that didn't get her free, she hollered rape. I had to give her neck a little squeeze.

She went out like a snuffed candle and I tossed her over my shoulder to take to the monks' mill, like the abbot said. When we got there, I tied one of her ankles to the millstone. Gave her plenty of leash, though, so's she could move around a bit once she came to. For thanks she called curses down on my head.

Aelfreda was fair-haired, middling tall, and maybe thirty years old. Younger than I expected and, ugly talk or no, a whole lot grander. Even in a rough peasant's cloak and mended tunic, she held herself as straight and proud as the dowager queen of England. Who might just have envied the way Aelfreda could make a man tall as me feel like he was being looked down on.

But she sure didn't talk like any queen. In a raw squawk, she said, "You're some kinda fool, know it? How long you think it's gonna be 'fore Lord Stanfeld busts me outta here?"

When I shrugged, her grey eyes raked across me like wind off the northern sea. "Stanfeld," she said. "Or sump'n else."

"Unh-hunh," said I.

"Don't believe me? Well, listen up."

She threw back her head and flung out her arms. "Come on, you elves," she cried. "Shoot him in the belly, turn him into jelly. Shoot him in the foot, turn him into soot."

Superstitious Sassenach! The English think the world's chock full of wicked little elves. You can't see 'em, 'course. But they're around, don't you know, just waiting to put an arrow in your back, give you all kinds of devilish diseases.

"Shut up about your silly elves," I said. "'Even if they exist—which I doubt—they're not near as bad as the Ellyllon, like we got in Wales. Ellyllon, now, they'll chew your bones and suck up your soul and swallow you down entire."

Aelfreda's lip curled in contempt for such foreign foolishness.

I said, "Anyways, elves can only jump Sassenachs."

Which is what I've always heard. Still, you never know and I was glad for the charm pouch that hung around my neck. It contained lupine and bishopwort and a sliver of St. Veronica, all of 'em fine protection against elves. And whatever else might be roaming around just out of mortal sight.

"So I ain't much impressed by your big talk and your doll-baby magic," I said as I went to the millhouse door. "There's no Welshman would be."

But Aelfreda wasn't done yet. "I can call sump'n besides elves, you know. I can call down powers. Powers and principalities."

"Sure you can," I said, giving her the old Welsh counter. "Thing is, will they come?"

For a while I didn't think the king's reeve would come, either. Took the man damn near a fortnight. Meantime, evil returned to Bracknel. Two days after I caught Aelfreda, the monks found a whole hare bled out right at the church-house door.

It sure wasn't Aelfreda's doing. Not unless she really could call down powers—or make herself invisible like witches always claim they can. But I figured there was a better explanation, one closer to hand.

I waited till that afternoon to see Abbot Hylltun, till after he'd finished exorcising the hare. Found him in the workyard behind the chapter house, sitting in a wicker chair and carving out new pens. Beside him was a small table littered with inkpots, parchment, trimmed goose quills. At his feet lay the black cat, asleep in the sun.

"Got a problem," I said.

"Indeed you do," he said. He picked up one of the quills and with a little knife set to paring its end into a nib. "So do we both. At least until Aelfreda is in her grave."

"It's about Aelfreda that I got the problem," I said.

The abbot cut a slit up the middle of the nib.

"This is what I'm thinking about the evil here at Bracknel," I said. "Item one: all the blood and guts, all the dead things, turn up inside the cloister. But the dolls were left at the gate, outside the cloister. Right?"

Abbot Hylltun nodded and I went on. "Item two: There's been innards and stuff found any number of different times. But just two dolls, both of 'em recent."

The abbot pressed the nib against the tabletop and, with a flick of his knife, squared it off. Then he set knife and new pen aside. "Continue," he said.

"Item three: Think back to before I came—no innards, no image, nothing at all turned up when somebody was watching the gate and guarding the walls. In other words, once regular watches started, the nastiness stopped cold. For what, a whole month? Until—"

"Until Brother Boda found a clump of guts in the bell tower. That's when I sent for you."

"Didn't you tell me there was a terrible storm the night before he found the guts? A storm bad enough to drive the guards inside?"

The abbot nodded.

"See where I'm headed? I think Aelfreda's witchiness ain't all that's going on here at Bracknel. Oh, she did the dolls. But, like I said, they were both left outside the gate."

I stopped to take a good look at the abbot, see if he was with me. He was fingering his sharp little knife.

I said, "Aelfreda couldn't have got inside the walls, not with half the monastery watching. And once I got here, there were only dolls left—outside."

"Well, she certainly could have gotten in during that storm, when the guards were out of the way."

"But that was just the once, right?"

Abbot Hylltun's eyebrows shot up. "Are you trying to say

something else is getting past our walls and bringing its evil to our doorstep?"

"Not necessarily getting past your walls," I said. "'Cause it wasn't something left that hare by the church. It was somebody."

Whilst the abbot sat staring at me, I let my own gaze rove round the cloister yard, from the turnip patch to the latrine to the chapter house itself.

"By St. Benedict," he said. "You can't mean someone right inside the monastery is responsible for this evil."

"Think over what I been telling you. It has to be one of the brethren."

The little abbot leaped out of his chair and marched right up to me. "There is no Judas here," he hissed. "God's soldiers don't turn traitor."

Abbot Hylltun might not have been very big, but he could cast a cold eye with the best of 'em. And now he cast it on me. "You, Welshman, are like as a lion that is greedy of his prey," he said, quoting the psalm. "It was you who killed that hare and left it at the church door."

"Me? What in hell for?"

"Because you aren't satisfied with what the monastery will pay you for Aelfreda. Don't think I didn't know all about you when I hired you. You're a thief—a relic thief, a man who steals from holy church. And now you're trying to squeeze money out of us with this false show of evil."

"Pretty good plan," I said. "Sure wish I'da thought of it. But I was guarding Aelfreda the night Brother Boda found that hare."

The abbot shot me another cold glower, then raised his face and his arms up in the air. "Here is the young lion lurking," he sang out. "Arise, O Lord, disappoint him, cast him down with thine own sword."

That, thought I, is the second time somebody's up and sicced the unseen on me. Maybe I better get out of here. Quick-like, too. Lest third time's the charm.

"I tell you, Welshman, once and for all," Abbot Hylltun said. "There is no traitor, there is no Judas at Bracknel."

He said it in his best pulpit tone. Then all of a sudden his eyebrows started twitching and he stopped talking. Presently, in a voice so low it was barely a whisper, he said, "A red-haired man is ever a curse."

I wondered what he meant by that. I didn't have red hair. Judas Iscariot did, though. And Brother Boda, too.

In spite of Aelfreda's elf threats and what Abbot Hylltun told God about me, I didn't leave the monastery after all. The abbot decided he'd got it wrong—decided I wasn't the problem at Bracknel. We both knew it was Aelfreda, didn't we? She could pull all manner of devil-tricks, couldn't she? You'd accept a raise in your pay for staying on as her guard, wouldn't you? The logic of his argument persuaded me.

So who was the problem at Bracknel? Not Lord Stanfeld. He never came to rescue Aelfreda, never helped her out at all. Nor was the reason hard to find.

Seems the king's reeve stopped at Stanfeld Hall on his way to the monastery. Told Stanfeld that King Ethelred's Witan—his council of thanes and bishops—had heard about the trouble at Bracknel. Said they hoped it didn't have anything to do with Ethelred's plan to give King Wood to the monks. Said Stanfeld should go see the king in Winchester real soon, bring his property deeds with him, Ethelred wanted to review some boundary markers twixt his land and Stanfeld's.

When the king's reeve—his name was Wulfsige—and his men arrived at Bracknel, he let Abbot Hylltun know this trial wasn't the only one he had on his docket. Nor was it the most important. "So start ringing your bells right now," Wulfsige said. "The king's justice will be done tomorrow morning at the monastery gate."

By first light, every peasant in the countryside—male and female, young and old, lame and whole—stood at the gate. It was a raw day even for February and the churls, wrapped in thin cloaks and blowing on cold fingers, could've made themselves busy inside. There was barley to be threshed and good ale to be brewed. But that was work and it didn't have to be done on court day. Lucky, then, that thereabouts court day came but maybe once in a decade. More often and the ground would've gone unploughed, the chickens unplucked, the beans unpicked. The whole countryside would've happily starved, so much good fun was the king's justice show.

"Ooh" they went when the monastery gate opened and a monk brought out bench and chair. "Ah" they went when Wulfsige sat down behind the bench. Then came "oh" as the monks gathered in the gateway and "ha" for the abbot's cat as he leaped atop the wall. But when I brought Aelfreda up from the mill-house, there was nary a sound at all.

I stationed her before the bench, close enough so Wulfsige could see her and she him—but not close enough so she could all of a sudden go for his eyes like she had several guards several times. Just to make sure she didn't act up, I carried a shepherd's crook. Its business end was around her neck.

This was the first time Wulfsige had seen our witch and he gave her a good studying. What he thought of her, I couldn't say—he had one of those faces that never changes, not for love nor money neither. As for Aelfreda, she looked like she'd love to stick a nail right between his legs.

Wulfsige spoke to her in a voice loud enough for everybody to hear. "This is the law concerning witchcraft and sorcery and secret acts of murder," he said. "If the accused cannot deny the charge, he—or she—is to forfeit his life."

Aelfreda said, also in a good big voice, "I never done it."

And she was no dummy to say that. In English law if you admit to a thing, you're dead within the week. Strung up at a crossroads with the pipes playing and the crowd cheering. Deny it and you can be fooling with dolls till you're eighty.

So, under English law, once Aelfreda cried her innocence, it didn't matter that I had all but caught her in the act. Her kin, maybe even Stanfeld himself, would supply oath-helpers to swear she'd done nothing wrong. Then the Crown would bring in its own oath-helpers to swear just the opposite.

But the king's reeve was no dummy, either. Why waste everybody's time with a case sure to end in a draw? "It appears," he said, "that we are unlikely to reach a true judgement. As a result, and according to the law, the defendant will undergo the three-fold ordeal."

The crowd heaved a happy Ahhh. Here came the real fun.

See you, the three-fold ordeal's the endmost step in the legal process, the one that offers up God's own proof in the matter. It'd go this way—first, Aelfreda'd have to stick her arm in boiling water. Then, if she was innocent enough not to blister, she'd move on to picking up three pounds of red hot iron and carrying it for nine feet.

15

If she still didn't blister, the only thing left was to get dunked. They'd put a rope around her middle and throw her into deep water. If she sank it meant the water accepted her and she was innocent. If she floated up, the water had rejected her. Her guilt was proved beyond a reasonable doubt.

"However," Wulfsige said, "in the interest of an expeditious proceeding, I will permit the defendant to waive the ordeal's initial phases."

At the bottom of that load of Latin was a real surprise— Aelfreda wouldn't have to risk cooking an arm or roasting her hands. She'd only have to do the ordeal by water. Which might seem like she was getting off easy. Except women-witches always come floating up.

Aelfreda must've known so, too. When the reeve said she'd be put to the water test, she lost her calm at last. She let out a squeal and her face went all mottled and green. But her legs stayed under her and by the time Wulfsige's men led her down to the millpond, she moved with the bold grandeur of a queen going to her coronation.

The crowd tumbled after her, churls, monks, me—and now a man mounted on a bay horse. Lord Stanfeld had come after all.

He was dark for an Englishman, with wild black hair and eyes like hot tar. At the pond he sat scowling atop his horse whilst the churls, his own and others, came up to him and bowed and scraped and knuckled their forelocks. The monks acted like he wasn't there. They moved to the far side of the pond, faces hid deep inside their black hoods.

Nor did Aelfreda make any sign that she saw Stanfeld, just stood quiet on the muddy mill path whilst Wulfsige's men wound her up in a rope, neck to knee to ankle. When they were done, she asked if she could kiss St. John's shinbone. It belonged to the monastery and was one of the holiest relics in all England.

Since the law said defendants could swear on a relic if they wanted, Wulfsige told Abbot Hylltun to have it brought down from the church-house. The abbot told Wulfsige he didn't care what the law said, no witch was coming anyplace close to John's sainted shin. After that I only heard a couple of more words—wood was one, I think, and king—until the abbot all of a sudden ordered Prior Cole to go and fetch St. John.

I don't know if Aelfreda blasphemed by swearing her innocence over the relic, like folks claimed she did. All I heard was Wulfsige command his men to toss her in the pond. She hit the water with a hard plunk.

An Arab leech I knew down in Sicily once told me there's no woman in the world won't bob right back up when she's dropped in a pond. Said it's because women are empty vessels. A man'll go straight to the bottom, so weighty is his soul.

But Aelfreda, alone of all her kind, must've been soul to the brim. When Wulfsige's men heaved her in the water, she sank like a rock. And, to further prove her case, she stayed sunk.

Everybody stood staring as the water of the pond grew still. Until finally Lord Stanfeld drew his sword and said in a loud voice, "God's judgment has been rendered. Set the woman free."

Wulfsige shrugged, then signaled to his men. They hauled her up.

The churls went wild. And why not? They'd seen a thing so wondrous rare they'd be talking about it into the millennium. Meantime, they leaped and danced and crowed and cried. One or two even fell in the millpond themselves. Then they wrapped Aelfreda in a thick wool blanket and chaired her home like she was Judith with the head of Holofernes in her hands.

"Congratulations!" I yelled as she went by, and gave her a big thumbs up. In reply she gave me a regal nod and the finger.

What passed amongst Stanfeld and Wulfsige and Abbot Hylltun, I don't know. But none of 'em looked very pleased as they spoke each to the other. Presently, Stanfeld rode one direction and Wulfsige another, with the abbot casting a cold eye after both.

It was time for me to be off, too. And time to collect my pay. I'd brought in the local witch, after all, just as I was hired to do. So, whilst abbot and prior were still at the millpond with the rest of the monks—shaking their heads and clucking and tch-tching and saying how shocked they were at the way things'd turned out—I went to wait in the abbot's lodge.

Its door hung open a crack and when I stepped inside, my foot crunched down on a sparrow head. Nor was that all. Around the empty cloister, I found a gutted newt on the chapter house step and, in the kitchen, two mutilated mice.

So, thought I, the millpond gave true justice. Just like I figured, Aelfreda never did the dirty at Bracknel.

Trouble was, anybody else could have. Well, maybe not the

abbot. Not today, anyhow. I'd had him in view for the entire afternoon, standing right beside Wulfsige, handing him St. John.

But Prior Cole had gone to fetch the relic—and taken his sweet time doing it, too. He could've planted the wicked things then. Or any other time for that matter: Abbot Hylltun wasn't the only one with a private cell and felt night shoes. As for why—well, Cole didn't like the abbot, maybe even had an eye to taking his place. Which might just happen if he could make Hylltun look bad enough to the other monks.

But maybe somebody else had the same idea. Brother Boda'd made it pretty clear he'd be happy to see the last of abbot and prior. On top of that, he was known to wander around at night and today I sure hadn't taken a count of the black hoods down at the millpond.

Then there was Stanfeld. He'd still be smarting under those threats by the king's reeve, maybe hurting enough that he'd want to show the monks their problems weren't over yet. Besides that, he'd come to the trial late. He could've easily snuck into the empty monastery whilst everybody else was at the millpond.

The notion of the monastery's being empty made me think back to the morning—when the abbot'd had to push his way through all the monks standing in the monastery gateway. Did he linger in the cloister so he could set out the dead stuff? He could've, that was for sure. But why on earth would he want to?

Well, thought I, it ain't my problem. And to be sure nobody tried to make it so, I got a shovel, scooped up the newt and the mice and the sparrow head, dumped 'em down the latrine. I figured I'd be long gone before there'd be any more around.

'Course, I was wrong again. Back in the abbot's lodge, a headless rat, still warm and twitching, lay on the oak table.

This time, though, I saw who left it there.

He made a bolt for the door. But I was closer and slammed it shut. Not a smart move. Now I stood in the dark with a killer who could stalk his prey even at night. And besides that, he was armed to the teeth.

I stripped off my cloak and twisted it around my arm and hand as protection against his sharp weapons. Then, summoning up all my courage, I advanced toward the corner where he lay in wait.

He was even bigger than I remembered, his eyes greener as they narrowed down in his blood-stained face. "Give it up, brother," I said. "You know you ain't got a whisker of a chance, not in this little bitty room."

With a snarl, he lunged for me. With a grunt, I grabbed at him. Missed, both of us, and the chase began.

Wall to wall we went, corner to corner. Down came the abbot's bookcase, over fell his chair. We swung from the rafters, we skittered on the floor. We dashed and darted, leaped and bounded and sprang.

Then he shot across the oak table, me right behind. Only he landed on his feet, but I hit square on my nose. I heard the crunch, felt the pain, tasted the blood.

I stood up and faced him. "That's it, you son of Satan," I hissed.

Then I pounced.

Snatched him up by his black tail and gave it a hard twist. You bet he clawed me. Bit me, too. But he calmed down quick enough, once I had him wound tight in my cloak. Cats are way too smart to fight to the death.

And so am I. That's why, when the abbot refused to pay up, I didn't fight about it. Didn't turn a hair when he claimed I hadn't caught a witch. Kept nice and quiet when he said, "After all, Aelfreda was found innocent of the charge. And as for my cat being some kind of witch, now really—"

I didn't fight him at all, just went and said a prayer in the church-house. Then I got on my horse and headed home.

But, see you, there's more than one way to skin a cat. Safely at rest in my saddlebag lay the shinbone of St. John.

The End

Received Mystery Writers of America's Robert L. Fish Memorial Award for Best First Short Story (2001).

SCABS

First morning of the strike, us girls line up outside of Standard Shirt's front gate. My teeth are chattering. And not just with the cold, though my brother Mick's lent me his mackinaw and I've got thick wool socks under my galoshes.

Nor am I the only one who's cold and trembly. We know we've got our gall to go on strike right now, it being winter and Mr. Roosevelt in office not even a year. So all forty-three of us seamstresses are scared, you can bet on it, staring through the chain fence while the company bulls slap their billy clubs against their palms. Helen Arena is wringing her hands and praying in Sicilian. And even big, tough Mary O'Faolain, who's been known to take a skillet to her husband's head when he comes home fighting drunk, looks pale as the snow she stands in.

About eight o'clock, Mr. Bell, the manager, comes out on the office porch. As usual, he's wearing the black topcoat and grey fedora he thinks make him look like a Chicago gangster. "Yez got ten minutes to get back inside and start working," he yells at us. He doesn't have the guts to come to the fence.

Lizzie Larosa, the union steward, walks up to the gate and says, "We ain't going to do that till we get what's right."

She says it a lot politer than I would if Mr. Bell had ever called me a goddam dago bitch like he did Lizzie not more than a month back.

"Awright, my dear—" When he's not cussing us, Mr. Bell talks down to us. "Then we'll find somebody who is willing to work," he says and hops back in his nice warm office.

Scabs, he means. We stand around the rest of the day waiting for them.

Lizzie and Mary and me gather up pieces of coal and cardboard to make a fire. Then we warm our hands and sing a few union songs. Around noon Mary's ma and Mrs. Sampson, the Methodist preacher's wife, and some others bring us sandwiches.

Don Tinker cruises past in his sheriff's car, John Barrymore profile on prominent display as usual. He looks surprised when he sees his cousin Lorraine's with us. He rolls down the car window and yells, "Thought you had better sense, Lorraine."

Then he sees me. "And you, Sally Jenkins. Ain't you too good for a picket line, now you decided to go to college?"

I don't say anything back, 'specially when I know lots of the girls agree with him. That's because when Standard Shirt opened a factory in our town and I got a job sewing hems, I made the mistake of saying it mightn't be for long, I might go to college. I don't know if I will or not and I joined the union, but some people still think I'm a snot, maybe even a company spy. Anyway, not to be trusted.

Now, though, Mary O'Faolain tells Don where to go. He drives away, laughing.

In the afternoon, Jack Zimanski, the union rep, finally gets down from Cleveland and he and Lizzie give speeches about being brave and sticking together no matter what.

No scabs show up that day, so come quitting time, we plant our picket signs in the snow piles by the fence and go home. First thing I do is ask Ma if I can put my feet on the stove rail. It's something she never lets us do no matter how cold we are, but this time she gives me a grin and a kiss and says go ahead. Criminey, my feet feel good on there.

"Tomorrow don't forget to take extra undies for when you go to the pokey," Ma says.

She's joking and not joking both, 'cause she knows what can happen on strike. Like when you beat up a scab crossing the picket line. She'd probably be mad if I didn't bust some strikebreaker's chops. And Pop? He'd plant a big kiss on me if I did and say, "Good for you, Sally girl. Their kind's nothing but animals. Got to have the sense beat into 'em, coming over here trying to take our jobs. Thump their butts bloody and ship 'em back to West Virginia, that's the ticket."

My family's been union since Knights of Labor days. And it's not been easy fighting owners able to buy up half the earth and scare hell out the other half. The Pinkertons killed my Ma's dad. Kicked open his head behind the roundhouse right after he shut down his locomotive and turned out for the Strike of '97. And I don't know how many times the yard bulls have beat up Pop and my uncles for holding railroad Brotherhood cards. When I was a little girl, carrying Pop's lunch bucket up to the picket line in '22, the National Guard stuck their guns right in my face and stole the boloney sandwiches.

But even with all that behind me, I have to admit I thought we shouldn't go out when we did, middle of a Depression. It'd be easy for the company to bring in scabs and dangerous for us if they did.

Lots of folks said we were lucky to have jobs at all, 'specially since most of us are women and working when a lot of men aren't. Said all we had to do was look around town, see 'em ten o'clock in the morning, idle on the street corner. A man like Joe Tully, best bricklayer in two counties my Pop always says. But Joe hasn't had work in pert'near a year, him with three little ones at home and a sick wife. I pass him lots of times over town, big red hands stuck in his overall pockets like he's ashamed of them for not having a trowel to hold. How long would it be before he crossed our picket line? And a hundred just like him. Good workers with hungry families.

Another thing against a strike was being without a paycheck Lord only knew how long. Maybe forever. So much for college. But would a college graduate even need to go on strike? It all made me so worried I was waking up nights freezing cold and sweating at the same time. I began to think maybe when the time came to vote on the strike, I'd vote nay.

Then I brought myself up short. I had the right to a living wage. And so does everybody else, though sometimes you have to fight for it. My family's always fought for it, gone hungry and bare-ass while the likes of Deputy Don Tinker is eating regular and his new wife strutting around in patent-leather shoes.

So in the end I vote to go out. How can I do other and still hold my head up at home or with the Local?

Later that first night, when they come off their runs, Pop says he's proud and Mick slaps me on the back. After supper, Grandpa limps over the way and gives me his lucky penny. Says he carried it in '09 and let Pop take it in '22 and Jamesy up there in the mill in Pittsburgh one time, too. Says he never thought he'd have to hand it to one of his granddaughters but he guesses times are changing and maybe they ought to.

I sleep good for the first time in three months.

Two days later the scabs come.

We watch as they climb off the company trucks in front of the gate. Forty of them, all women and, by their looks, from the mountains. From West Virginia, most likely. I'd hoped they'd be city girls, tough cookies with some swagger to them and a screw-you attitude. But the quivery things crawling down from the flatbeds are like a gang of female scarecrows they're so ragged and skinny. And after the trucks pull away, they look scared as rabbits with their feet in a trap.

But the dumb hillbillies are after our jobs. They deserve what's coming to them.

When the gate opens to let the scabs in, we form up like we planned—a horseshoe in front of it, triple deep to keep them from getting around us. And like we planned, they march right down the middle. We don't give any warning shout, just close in behind and swarm all over them.

That's when the screaming starts, the cussing, too, and the fighting. It's like we're drunk. Or crazy maybe. We use pick handles on them and bricks and blackjacks made out of socks filled with bird shot. We use our fists, too, if we don't have anything else.

I have a crowbar stuck down my mackinaw, but I never swing it. One of the company bulls wrenches the thing off me and tosses it over the fence. Then he goes after Lizzie and her brick. So I start using my fists just like Pop showed Mick and Jamesy when they were little fellows and me watching from the shed roof.

I bang one girl's nose so hard it blooms blood like a big red rose. She grabs hold of it and runs like hell. All the way back to West Virginia, I expect. After that, Mary O'Foalain and me corner a scrawny blonde against the company fence. We kick her till Mary says we better stop before we kill her. But I feel like I've been drinking 'shine out of a quart jar.

"She's nothing but a goddam scab," I say, then kick her again. I don't quit till she falls in a snow drift and leaves off her screaming.

Us strikers would've won. We've drawn enough blood and broke so much bone the company won't find a scab fit to work. But presently the high sheriff shows up with every single deputy in this end of the county. Oh, we have the wind up by then and are willing to fight the law, too. Only they have guns. That sobers me off pretty quick. I do respect a shotgun, specially when the barrel's against my throat.

They make us put our hands on top of our heads and watch the scabs pass through the gate and onto the work floor. Then they tell us to sit down while they put handcuffs on. Lizzie Larosa spits in a deputy's face when he clips on the cuff and I'm gobbing up a good one for mine, too. But then I see he's Tommy Young who I went eight grades of school with. I just call him a dirty name.

They spread us all over the county. Me and Mary and Lizzie and a dozen others—Jo Roark and her sister Peg are among them—go to the town hall, where the jail is. But the jail's already so crowded the only place left is the cold, bare meeting room on the third floor. That's where they put us, along with half a dozen scabs who got confused and jumped on a deputy.

Jo and Peg shouldn't be there. They aren't on strike, aren't even working because they're both pg, which the company found out and made them quit. They were just bringing us coffee when the law scooped them up along with everybody else. I try to tell Tom Young that but he says it's out of his hands till their husbands get off work and can come with a lawyer or bail or whatever. And that probably won't be before morning.

"Ain't that just a crying shame," a scab says. She's a tall redhead with one eye already puffed up purple and knuckles scraped enough to look like she gave as good as she got.

She sounds pretty smart alecky, so Mary asks her if she wants a matched set of shiners. She knows she's outclassed and outgunned. She doesn't make any answer, just goes and sits in the back of the room by herself.

The rest of the hillbillies are huddled in a corner and we take to staring at them like a copperhead ready to strike. After a bit, Lizzie says maybe we ought to sing to them. She wants to sing something called "The Internationale." But since nobody except her knows the words, we launch into "We Shall Overcome." When the scabs just stare down at the floor, we start on "Solidarity Forever," see if that'll rile them some.

But 'cause of its tune, they think we're singing "Battle Hymn of the Republic" and join in with the regular words. First thing you know, everybody's belting out "Little White Lies" and "A Million

25

Dollar Baby in the Five and Dime." We spend the next hour warbling like birds in a gilded cage and end up with the old-time hymns. One little hillbilly girl sings "Bringing in the Sheaves" sweet enough to carry every one of us straight into heaven. And her with a broken nose.

Then the sheriff's men get tired of it and tell us to shut up.

They leave Don Tinker in charge.

First thing he does is give his cousin Lorraine a blanket. The Tinkers are clannish as wolves and about as mean. Which is why she takes it, the hell with the rest of us.

"Guess you think I oughtta give you something, too, little Miss College," Don says to me.

Don's never liked me. Mary says its 'cause I wouldn't go out with him in high school. But he never asked. Just called me a stuck up . . . well, never mind a stuck up what.

Now, I ignore him.

Lorraine wraps herself in the blanket, then goes to crouch by the fire escape door. We call her nasty names and Mary, fists balled, heads after her. But Lizzie says leave her be, union members have to stick together no matter what.

The scabs aren't so forgiving. They start screeching again about it not being fair they're in jail and they want to go home. We tell them to shut up and grow up.

Don, who's meantime been laughing his butt off, says we better behave ourselves or else. Then he goes downstairs to drink coffee and congratulate himself on being a tough lawman and a good kinsman, too.

Later, Jo Roark decides she needs a cigarette and since the bulls grabbed our smokes soon as we came through the door, we naturally look to the scabs. For some reason they got to keep their tobacco and now they're puffing up a storm.

We ask them to share. They tell us what we can do to ourselves. We say what we're going to do is take their tobacco.

Hearing that, they set up a high old yowling. But it doesn't stop Mary and Lizzie and me. We wade straight into them, Mary popping noses right and left, Lizzie biting and scratching like a cat in heat. I go for the red-haired scab, fixing to snare the pack of tailormades I spot in her coat pocket.

Four deputies rush up the steps, Don Tinker in the lead.

"There's too goddam much commotion in here," he yells.

The bulls grab whoever they can. They toss us around like medicine balls 'til all us union girls and a couple scabs are lined up against the wall with three pistols pointed our way.

Don gives me a hard rap on the head. He doesn't touch the red-haired scab, though she's right next to me and cussing to make a hoor blush.

When he finds out the fight was over tobacco—those hillbillies couldn't wait to blab—he tells us all, union and scab both, to hand it over. All of it, along with our rolling papers and the redhead's Luckies.

"Ladies shouldn't be smoking anyhow," he says like he's some kind of Methodist deacon. "Gimme your matches, too, all of yunz."

Another deputy takes off his cap and like good little girls the scabs throw their stuff into it.

Us union women don't make a move.

Don glares at us a while before he says, "Gimme your makings and your matches right now or I'll strip yunz nekkid."

"You and who else?" Jo Roark says, sticking her round face right in his.

He can see Jo's expecting. Anybody can. But he gives her a shove in the chest and the only reason she doesn't fall down is 'cause Lizzie and one of the scabs catch her first.

A red curtain drops in front of my eyes like it always does when I get mad. I hear myself growl out loud and I know I'm going to kill Don Tinker. But Lizzie grabs me by the arm and keeps me from it.

"He ain't worth you do more time," she says. "Now everybody, give the man your stuff. We outta here soon as Mr. Zimanski comes with the bail."

So, Lizzie being who she is, we all hand over our smokes. Even Lorraine.

Don gives Lorraine a big grin. She's got no better sense than to return it. I shoot her a loud raspberry.

After Don's boys have everything stuck in a paper bag, he points at me and the red-haired scab. "You two are coming with me."

Lizzie starts hollering that if anything happens to me, she'll have his badge. He just laughs.

Downstairs, he throws us in a cell barely bigger than a broom closet. The only light and air come through a barred window in the iron door. But at least it's warm and we can shed our coats.

"I'll tend to yunz later," Don says, then locks us in and goes away.

I'm not surprised at him pulling a stunt like this. He probably knows I'm scared the rest of the girls will think I'm a traitor like Lorraine. And he knows I won't relish being with the scab. Wouldn't he be surprised to find out that right now I'm just too tired to care?

The scab doesn't look like she feels any too good, either. So we stretch out on our coats and watch the paint peel off the ceiling. Presently, she says, "I'm hongry."

I tell her I don't want to hear about it.

She shrugs and turns her bruised eyes back to the ceiling.

Well past noon, Mrs. Logue, the town constable's wife, brings us a mess of fried potatoes and eggs, then stands and gawks at us.

"How we s'pose to eat this?" I ask when I see there's no knife nor fork nor spoon.

Mrs. Logue doesn't say anything, only gives me a jail house look.

"Reckon she thinks we'd use 'em on each other 'stead of the vittles," the scab says.

She grins at me. I don't grin back.

The food's greasy and cold, but I stuff it down fast as I can seeing how I have to use my fingers. The scab does the same, then we both lick our plates.

"How 'bout some coffee," I say to Mrs. Logue when we hand her back the plates.

"And some matches," the scab says, pulling a filthy sack of Gold Flake out from the neck of her dress. "That boss of your'n took our matches away."

"He ain't no boss of me," Mrs. Logue says and marches off down the hall.

But it turns out she's got a heart after all. Before long she opens the cell door and comes in carrying two cups of coffee and a box of matches. "Keep 'em," she says. "They let the boys smoke in here, even when they're drunk. Don't see why yunz can't."

The scab mumbles a word of thanks and takes her coffee and the matches. But I'm not thanking a hack, even if we do go to the same church. I grab the coffee and throw myself back down on the floor. Mrs. Logue gives me another of her looks and locks us up tight.

The coffee's strong and hot. I sip it while the scab peers into her tobacco sack, then jams her hand in the pocket of her dress. "Shoot," she says when she doesn't find what she wants.

I pull out the folder of cigarette papers I wasn't about to let the laws steal from me. "Guess you'll have to share this time, hillbilly, if you want a smoke," I say, waving the papers at her.

She stares at me a long minute, then sticks her hands up in the air like somebody getting captured in a Tom Mix movie. "You got me, pard," she says with another grin and forks over the Gold Flake.

When we get our cigs rolled and lit, we sit on the floor with our backs against the wall, smoking in silence. Finally, I can't stand it anymore. I've just got to ask. "How come you want to take my job away?"

She's quiet so long I figure she's not going to answer. But when she finishes her cigarette, she drops it in the tin cup and says, "Didn't come to take your job. I don't even know you."

Dumb hillbilly. 'Course she doesn't know me. "Take our jobs, I mean," I explain like to a little baby.

"I come 'cause my daddy took sick in his lungs and couldn't get no crop in last year. I butchered our pig in November, but it's done et up now. 'Cept for some lard, which is all the little'uns got to take to school in their lunch pails. When they's able to go to school a'tall. My mama and my sister Ruby and me had to feed them boys. And we didn't know how we was going to do it even though we prayed over it ever' night."

She starts to twist a hank of red hair. Her dress is so worn you can see her nipples." Then last week a man come up the hollow in a big black car wanting to know if anybody around needed work. Said if they did, be at the Philippi Bridge Tuesday morning, sun up. Come Monday noon, I started in walking. Got there just past midnight, slept the rest of the night on a pallet in a big shed with all them other girls. Some been travelling since after church on Sunday, they told me. Then just like the man said, right when the light come over top the trees two flatbeds pulled up and all us girls climbed onto 'em and before long we was in Ohio."

I give her a hard look, seeing if it's true. And when I know it is, I can't think of anything to say.

"When we rolled up in front of y'all's company, we didn't have no notion what was going on. I seen y'all standing out in front, but I

figured you was there same reason we was. You was hongry. Sure
didn't expect to get beat on."

When she finishes, I think about Ma and Pop and Mick and
Jamesy and me sitting at the kitchen table Sunday noons eating Ma's
roast, a little gravy leaking out of its boat onto the oil cloth.

"I'm Iola Fountain," she says. "You got a name, too, I reckon."

Which I'm not about to give to any scab, feel sorry for her or
not. I reach for the Gold Flake.

We're just finishing our ciggies when Tom Young opens the cell
door. "Yunz are going back upstairs."

He doesn't say why and we don't ask, though we figure Don
Tinker's finally off duty.

In the attic, Iola joins the hillbillies. She hands around tobacco
and some of my papers she went and filched. In return, she gets grins
and thanks.

I get nasty looks until Lizzie puts her arm around me. "This our
comrade," she says to the other girls. "Who knows what solidarity
means."

"Damn straight she does," Jo says and Mary starts in nodding.
But the rest still don't look too sure and I want to explain what
happened.

Lizzie says that's not necessary. "What's necessary now is we get
to pee."

She turns to Tom Young at the top of the steps. "Or you want
us to let loose where we stand?"

Tom stares at her. So do I. We've never heard Lizzie talk like
this before. Even as a kid, she was so ladylike she'd blush to her
toenails if anybody mentioned such things around her. Now here she
was talking like an old hobo. "We need to pee," Lizzie says again.
"Now."

Tom makes a quick decision. He hustles down the steps.

Presently, Mrs. Logue comes up. She has a bucket in each hand.
"Use these," she says.

Lizzie shakes her head. "There's lotsa girls won't go in public."

Mrs. Logue makes a face. "Tell that to the sheriff."

"Get him up here then."

But it's Don Tinker who eventually comes up the steps. "Yunz
can use the outhouse back of the town hall. But just a couple, three at
a time."

"Jo and Peg first 'cause they're expecting," Lizzie tells him. "Then the rest. I'll go last. But before the scabs, you can be damn sure."

"Hey, Mr. Sheriff-man," one of the scabs says in a whiney voice. "I'm expecting, too."

"Like hell," Jo says. "Or if you are, it's the imp of Satan in there."

"And we can take care of that quick enough," Mary says. "Fetch me a coat hanger."

Don tells Mary to shut up or she'll be spending time in the hole "like your old man when he gets feisty."

Then he says for Jo and Peg to go with Mrs. Logue. But they'll have to take the fire escape because by now every cell, office, and closet in the whole building, even the hallways, are packed with prisoners.

He sends the scab who claimed she was pg along with them. "The rest of yunz sit down and wait your turn."

As we light on the cold floor, Mary whispers, "At least Lorraine Tinker didn't get to go first."

After what seems like a week, the four return, complaining bitterly about the ice on the fire escape. "We coulda miscarried out there," Jo says. "Then, Don Tinker, you'da been the one with the gun to your head."

Don shrugs her off and tells Mrs. Logue she should take me and Lorraine next. "And that one," he says, pointing at Iola Fountain.

I feel like I've been shot. What must the girls think? What can they think about me and Lorraine and the scab? One of Lizzie's black eyebrows shoots up and even Mary looks a little funny about it.

Outside on the fire escape landing, we find we're at the top of three flights of wooden stairs nobody's cleaned the ice and snow off. The steps are narrow, too, and the rickety railing sags in places. Below lies a half-shoveled parking lot strewn with cinders.

When I complain Mrs. Logue says, "Them others made it just fine. And they expecting."

She waves at the marks on the steps. "Scoot along on your bottoms. That's what they done."

"And likely got ice slivers up their butts," Lorraine says. She puts both hands on the railing and begins to sidestep down.

Iola lingers a moment, then sets to sidestepping right behind.

I watch them slip a few times and decide to go down on my butt.

Mrs. Logue, who's shivering pretty good by now, says she can watch us through the window. "'Cause I know where you two live," she says to Lorraine and me. "And that'n won't run off in this weather."

She goes inside. Through the door I hear her and Don arguing about duty—it's his to take care of county prisoners, no it's hers in the town jail and wait'll the sheriff hears and don't be threatening me, Donald Tinker.

I'm just settling onto the top step when Iola loses her footing and slides into Lorraine.

Lorraine swings around and lets out a torrent of cuss words.

"Shut your filthy mouth," Iola tells her. "It's awful slick right here. I almost went over the rail."

"Sounds like a good idea, scab. Whyn't you lemme help you?" Lorraine says.

She gives Iola a good shove.

Iola shoves back.

The railing dissolves into ice shards and sawdust.

Lorraine screams all the way down.

I stare at her lying in the snow and cinders. All I can think is how much she looks like a mail sack tossed off the Pittsburgh Express.

What Iola thinks, I can't say. But she's shaking hard.

Don and Lizzie barrel onto the landing. "Stay inside," he orders everyone else and slams the door shut.

"What happened?" Don asks as he and Lizzie peer into the parking lot.

I hear men down there. They sound scared. "Jesus, Don," one yells up. "I think Lorraine's neck is broke."

Don glances from me on the top step to Iola by the broken railing. He hauls me up by my coat collar. "What in hell happened out here?" he hollers in my face.

Below, someone says, "She's dead."

Don's mouth twitches and when he speaks again his voice is low and mean. "I asked you what happened." His fist is against my throat.

I look past him at Iola. She's still shaking.

"Did the scab do something to Lorraine?" Lizzie asks.

I think about union folks sticking together. And how my family's always been union. I think about my brothers, Mick and Jamesy, good union men both.

I think about Iola's little brothers. And those lunch buckets with nothing but lard in them.

"If that hillbilly killed my cousin . . ."

I take a deep breath of air so cold it burns all the way down. "Lorraine slipped on the ice. The rail broke," I tell Don and Lizzie. "It was an accident."

I tell them that until they believe me.

***

When the strike ends, Iola and the other scabs go back to West Virginia.

I go to live in Cleveland.

The End

AFTER ALL THESE YEARS

"Grading English papers can give you the creeps," I told Jerry Schaeffer as we dug compost into central Wisconsin's sandy soil.

Jerry lives next door to me—Margaret Holmstad, retired English professor. Since I was new in town, he'd volunteered to help get my garden started.

"Didn't know student writing was so interesting," he said with a laugh.

"If you don't believe me," I said, "come inside when we're done. You can have a beer and take a look at what I'm grading."

"Is going in your house a good idea right now?"

Jerry's wife was out of town and the neighbors couldn't help but keep track of a man who stood six-four and sported a jaw full of white beard.

"There are some essays I want you to see," I said. "Disturbing papers."

I wanted Jerry to read them because he was a psychiatric social worker. Or, rather, he used to be. Then he won the lottery and became a full-time sculptor. But I knew even the most blissfully retired pro likes to keep a hand in.

That's why I work in distance learning. That and the money, of course. My own early retirement had nothing to do with the lottery. I'd just neglected important parts of my life for far too long. Now, a year later, I miss neither teaching nor living in California. A regular paycheck is another question.

After we decided my screen porch was within the pale of local morality, I brought Jerry a beer and the student papers. He stretched out on the chaise longue.

I sat next to him and said, "The writer's name is Eldred Bates."

Eldred had signed up for Pre-College Composition, though that didn't necessarily mean he was high school age. To enroll, he'd only had to supply name, address, social security number. Beyond that, there was no information on him.

Eldred's first assignment was a paragraph about his background, done in pencil on brittle, lined paper. He'd gotten the date right—May 25, 1996. And from among the rest of the smudges and scribbles, I'd gleaned that Eldred wasn't married and had no intention of ever being married. "*I have too much family value already,*" he wrote.

I returned the assignment with a note asking him to type his work and he complied without complaint.

"So what's the problem?" Jerry asked.

"Just read that how-to theme in your hand."

Eldred had written, "*It is easy to kill a whole family including the dog. All it takes is the right poison, the right time and family.*"

"Gets straight to the point, doesn't he?" Jerry said, then read on.

"*There's alot of different poisons out on the market. One can find many in their own home. Spot cleaner or in a fire extinguisher.*"

Jerry gave the page a disgusted rattle. "He's barely literate."

"Keep reading."

"*Cargon tet is the ingredient in those. It is not very good for a mass poisoning which is what you've got when you do your whole family. Its messy, people ~~puke~~ throw up and wriggle around on the floor. Viacor use to be ok. But you can't get it anymore even in rat poison. You have to shoot them on Thanksgiving before the game comes on. Nobody is probably drunk yet or just a little.*"

Jerry shook his head, then went on to a description of Eldred's home life. Half way through it, he said, "Sounds like anyone who wiped out this particular family would be doing a public service."

Eldred didn't use words like incest, infanticide, bestiality. He simply told a story—about a litter of puppies drowned along with an unwanted baby and about the old man who dug their bodies into his potato patch.

"Well?" I said when Jerry finished reading. "What's he trying to do? Shock me? Scare me?"

Jerry's brows creased together. "When I was in high school there was a family out in the country—"

He bit his lip to summon up the memory. "Killed on

Thanksgiving, three or four of them. Poor family. Lived in an old tarpaper house. No indoor plumbing."

"Poisoned?"

"Shotgunned. I remember kids making jokes like, 'What do you do with the trash on Thanksgiving? You blow it away.' "

"Who killed them?"

Jerry shrugged. "It happened years ago."

"Remember anything about a dog? Eldred mentions one."

"Part collie, part pit bull, people said. Mean as hell. The cops found it out in the potato bed, killed, too."

"Sounds a lot like the murder in Eldred's paper," I said.

"I could be wrong about what happened. It was a long time ago. And anyway, I went in service about then."

For a while he sat ruminating, then said, "I think on the one hand you're right. Eldred wants to shock you. But he also wants to please you by putting in lots of details, like you said to."

"But why details from a murder? This murder?"

"Probably because it was very big news for a very long time."

I was still disturbed. Could, in some strange way, this Eldred be stalking me? "Maybe I should find out more about the murders. I suppose the Post carried the story."

Jerry tossed away Eldred's theme. "Lighten up, Margaret. All your boy's guilty of is some petty yank-teach's-chain."

His tone made me feel better. "He doesn't sound like a homicidal maniac?"

"I don't know what a homicidal maniac is," Jerry said, putting a hand on my thigh. "But I do know about sex maniacs. Wanna meet one?"

So much for the screen porch as a citadel of chastity.

Despite Jerry's nonchalance, I wanted to know more about that family massacre. I called the *Post*.

"It happened on a cold Thanksgiving day about forty years ago," I told the publisher, another neighbor of mine.

"I do wish," she replied, "that you'd said you wanted me to research the subject, not recall it. But, yes, I remember those murders. Matter of fact, I got my first by-line on the story. Wasn't even out of college and—"

"Before you start your Kit Whalen, Girl Reporter, number, just give me the facts," I said, not exactly cutting off a rags-to-riches story. Kit's family had owned the *Post* since 1893.

"Come down to the office," Kit said. "Read about it and then, if you want, I'll tell you what Dad wouldn't print."

The next day I went to read about the Braun family.

THREE IN FAMILY MURDERED
Two Missing

Authorities are baffled by what Sheriff Charles Jackson calls the "gruesome" murders of three people in their Macon township farmhouse on Thursday.

Found shot to death were Cletus Braun; his wife, Frances; and Cletus's father, George.

Cletus and Frances's children, Naomi, 17, and Harold, 16, have not been found. Nor has a murder weapon.

Harold, I thought. Not so different from Eldred.

A rural mail carrier discovered the bodies Friday morning and the authorities as yet had neither motive nor suspects. The sheriff said it didn't look like robbery.

There were no signs of a struggle. George and Cletus Braun lay near the kitchen table, Frances Braun by the counter where she'd apparently been cutting pumpkin pie. Except for dessert, the Thanksgiving meal had been eaten.

Photographs showed a dilapidated, two-story farmhouse, sided in peeling tar paper. A battered pickup sat in the yard.

Below the pictures was a sidebar, by-lined Kit Whalen and headed "Brauns Still Lived In The 1930's."

The house and barn have electricity, but there is no indoor plumbing and Frances Braun cooked on a wood-burning stove. The family did not have a telephone or TV. Their only radio was a pre-war Bendix.

The Brauns recently quit farming and now rented their acreage to neighbors. Neither of the children went to school. Naomi worked at the Macon cheese factory and the Braun men hired out as farm laborers.

I thought about the two missing kids, Naomi and Harold. What kind of a life was it in that old house for a couple of teenagers? Awful enough to shoot their way out of?

The *Post* said that although a search was underway, Sheriff Jackson wouldn't speculate about where the kids were. "I don't know if they got kidnapped or killed or if they just scrammed out of there while the other murders were going on." He added that neither had a driver's license and the Brauns' truck, the family's only vehicle, was still on the premises.

That was Saturday. The *Post* didn't go to press on Sundays, even for the county's first murder in seven years and its only mass murder ever. But Monday's headlines announced the Brauns had been killed by shotgun.

Searchers had turned up neither the weapon nor Naomi and Harold. The family dog, though, was discovered in the garden, shot to death. They'd also found tire tracks that didn't belong to the Braun's pickup or the mailman or the neighbors. Puzzling, too, was that on a fifteen degree day, the Braun children had left their only coats in the house.

The story ran for weeks, with headlines like "Relatives Baffled. Services Held. Where Are Braun Children?" Finally, it disappeared. Not, however, before Sheriff Jackson opined that whoever killed the Brauns "was a crazy nut case."

When I finished reading, I joined Kit Whalen for coffee in her office. "You said you'd tell me something about the murders that your father wouldn't print."

Kit showed me to a chair, poured coffee, then sat behind her desk. She touched a hand to her hair. A new dye job had turned it more brass than gold. I was glad I'd stayed brunette.

"You mean the incest angle," she said. "Back in those days such things weren't mentioned in a small town newspaper. Which doesn't mean such things weren't discussed all over said small town."

"I got the impression no one knew the Brauns well enough to

accuse them of incest."

"You must've grown up in a big city, Margaret. Here in the boonies, we figure we know our neighbors well enough to accuse them of whatever we want."

Kit said town gossip had it that the year before, Naomi had been pregnant—by her brother.

"But," Kit added, "the Braun neighbors told me they doubted Harold could've screwed anybody, never mind make a baby."

Today, Harold might be called developmentally disabled or, more harshly, retarded. Back then, people still said "simple-minded" and "not right in the head."

"I don't think he was right physically, either," Kit said. "The neighbors said he looked more like twelve than sixteen."

"So was Naomi pregnant or not?"

"Nobody ever saw her with a baby."

"Was she retarded, too?"

"The neighbors didn't think so. They said she was just very quiet. Other than that, they didn't know much about her."

"Why not? The Brauns must've been living out there forever."

When Kit paused to light a cigarette, she didn't ask if I minded. That's what I like about rural Wisconsin—folks don't make apologies for deadly behavior.

"They'd only moved in a few years before," she said. "And they only worked the farm for maybe two years. Then farming must've gotten in the way of their drinking, so they decided to rent out the property. After that, they did just enough work to keep themselves in booze. Mostly, though, they lived off the rent and Naomi's wages at the cheese factory."

"Did the mother drink, too?"

"I don't know," Kit said. "Why are you so interested in this old business?"

I told her about my student's strange choice of subject matter. And that Jerry Schaeffer agreed it bore a resemblance to these murders.

"Dear Jerry," Kit said. "It's hard to believe he's become an artist. And before that, a social worker of all things. Jerry was one reckless kid way back when. He . . ."

She stopped. "But that was then. Now is a whole bunch better."

"Couldn't agree more," I said as I refilled our cups from the old drip coffee pot that bubbled evilly on a stand behind Kit.

"I didn't pursue the Braun story to its conclusion," I said. "Who killed them? And what happened to Naomi and Harold?"

"The murders have never been solved. Or I should say, the case has never been closed. But most everybody—the sheriff, anyway, and Dad, too—was pretty sure the kids did it. The only mystery is why they were never charged."

Kit paused to drink some coffee and light another cigarette, then said, "They turned up, finally, and I got an interview with Naomi. Did you see it?"

I shook my head.

"Didn't come to much. She told me the same story she told Sheriff Jackson. Dad talked to him a lot, by the way. Naturally none of it ever got printed."

Kit and I were still talking when her secretary interrupted us. There was a crisis that only Kit could resolve.

She squashed out her cigarette. "Duty calls. But we can talk again, if you want. And since you didn't read my interview with Naomi Braun, I'll bring a copy. Dad's old notebook, too."

After we agreed to meet the following day, Kit said, "I forgot to ask. Did Jerry tell you he used to date Naomi Braun?"

At home, I read another of Eldred's papers.

"*Farming is dangerous business,*" he wrote. "*There's things that can kill you everyday on the farm. You can get french fried by down lines or sucked up by a corn picker. The cows can crush you, the hay can drop onto you.*

"*You can be poison, too. Your mom might of canned botulism with the tomatoes. Or your grampa could of got confused out in the woods and brought home toadstools. There's so much danger laying around on a farm you would not believe it.*"

Eldred listed still more rural hazards, until he concluded with, "*There's lots of other dangerous jobs besides farming. On TV they tell about reporters in the battle zones and teachers all the time get shot. Certain ones ought to. Ha ha.*"

Was that a threat?

I decided it might be and Jerry needed to know about it. Right away.

His studio was in a building that once housed McCrory's Small Engine Repair. And with the blue sparks shooting out of the welding torch and hunks of metal scattered across the oil-stained floor, it still looked more engine shop than artist's atelier. But then Jerry was no effete modeler of clay or marble-chipping Michelangelo wannabe. He worked in steel beams.

When I shoved Eldred's paper at him, he turned off the torch and pushed back his welding mask. "Damn it, Margaret. Can't you see I'm busy?"

I convinced him to read the paper anyway. After he finished, he said, "So?"

"Eldred is threatening me."

Jerry sighed, then steered me to the little office area in back. There, from a file-drawer, he produced a bottle of Johnny Walker.

After a few pulls at the whiskey, I calmed down and we settled onto a pair of folding chairs.

"What'd you find out at the newspaper?" Jerry asked.

I told him what I'd read and heard, finishing with, "Kit said that one afternoon right before Christmas, the Braun kids walked into the sheriff's office. Just like that. Explained they'd been hiding in an empty cabin near Lake Downer.

"Oh sure," Jerry said. "In winter without coats. Or food, probably. And how'd they keep warm without anyone seeing smoke from this cabin's chimney?"

"I wondered that, too. But Kit claims there used to be cabins in the forest back of Lake Downer almost that hidden away. Summer cottages, but with kerosene heaters and pantries full of canned goods. Clothes, too, and lanterns. All the comforts of home."

"True enough," Jerry said. "So what'd the kids say about the murders?"

"The boy didn't say anything. He was absolutely incoherent and stayed that way. But Naomi claimed three men had shown up with a shotgun. She thought they were Indians."

Jerry rolled his eyes.

"Naomi said they wanted the Brauns' money."

Jerry laughed. "Money? The Brauns?"

I shushed him and continued with Naomi's story. "The men said they were from up north but they'd been passing through on Thanksgiving morning and stopped in a tavern. While they were there, they heard an old guy bragging about all the money he kept in his house. They must've found out his name and where he lived because that afternoon the three burst into the Brauns' kitchen in the middle of Thanksgiving dinner."

"Did anyone actually believe the girl?"

"Of course not. But, on the other hand, when the sheriff talked to the bar owner, it turned out three Indians really had been in the place on Thanksgiving."

"I remember that part. But nobody ever located them. Disappeared into the rez, I guess."

"You seem to remember quite a lot. For having been away at the time."

Jerry took another drink of whiskey, then said, "I went out with Naomi Braun a couple times. When we were Juniors. Took her to the movies. I've forgotten what we saw. All I remember is she was very quiet. Read a lot. Pretty, though. Dark hair, blue eyes. I probably would've asked her out again, but she quit school then. Don't think I ever saw her after that."

"Would you say she was capable of shooting her family?"

"God, Margaret. What a question. I never thought about it. Not from that day to this."

Something in Jerry's voice made me believe he knew more about Naomi than he was letting on. And what about all those psych classes he must have had to take, all the case studies he had to read, all the teenage killers he probably had to evaluate?

"Seems as if the sheriff or the D.A. or somebody could've wrung the truth out of her eventually," he said. "Or for sure out of her brother. I wonder why they weren't arrested. Held on suspicion or whatever."

"Kit said they probably would've been. Except all at once their grandfather's sister swept onto the scene. Apparently she had more money than God and more lawyers than Satan. After that, nobody could get anywhere near those kids."

"So," Jerry said, "since there wasn't any real evidence to hold them on, they walked."

"But where'd they walk to?"

"Nobody seemed to know. Or at least my buddies back here didn't. Out west someplace, I heard. I also heard the brother died not long afterward. Or maybe he got put in a home. I don't remember. It was a long time ago."

"Do you think—" I drew a deep breath. "He might not be dead?"

Jerry stood up. "Gotta get back to work," he said. And dismissed me with a kiss.

Next morning, I went to meet Kit at a cafe downtown. I was hardly inside before the waitress told me Kit was dead.

"Had a heart attack yesterday afternoon," she said. "And if that ain't enough to frost ya, last night somebody went and robbed her house."

There was nothing else to do but go home and work with Eldred's farm essay.

"In your most recent paper," I began, "you've neglected certain details of rural life. The farmhouse kitchen, for instance, which often served as kitchen, living room, gun room, and family entertainment center.

"Not that it was always very inviting. The farmhouse I'm thinking of had electricity, but its kitchen appliances amounted to wood-burning cook stove, dented refrigerator, and a hand pump attached to the zinc sink.

"Ragged green shades covered the windows and a single light bulb dangled from the ceiling on a frayed cord. The linoleum once had a pattern of pretty red and grey flowers. Now it was just grey."

I hit the Delete key—Eldred had served his purpose—and thought about what else had been in the kitchen. A scarred oak table and, if I remembered rightly, five pressed-wood chairs. An old floor-model Bendix radio, two easy chairs, and, under the gun rack, a sagging brown couch.

On that Thanksgiving, George Braun sat at the head of the oak table, a small man wearing a dirty red hunter's cap and a week's worth of grey beard. Across from him was his son, Cletus. They were the only ones at the table. Frances Braun ate standing by the stove, Naomi and Harold on the couch.

Both the children were tall, dark-haired, and rail-thin. One of Harold's pale blue eyes was swollen shut from the beating he'd taken earlier when he spilled an armload of firewood. Now, he and his sister were banished from the table because he'd spilled his milk.

"Oughtta make yas eat outside by the goddam dog," their father said. "Got no better manners'n that thing."

"Dog's smarter though," George Braun said with a drunken giggle.

He'd already been drunk when he came home from Parkos' Tap

44

at noon. "Bullshittin' Parkos says he's closing early cuz it's Thanksgiving. What's to be thankful for, I says. Go on home, Parkos says, eat some turkey, punkin pie, enjoy your family. Then he shoves me off the barstool and out the door, the bohunk bastard."

A plate of turkey and mashed potatoes sat in front of George. It hadn't been touched; the old man was drinking Thanksgiving dinner from a tumbler.

"That sure ain't the drink Parkos give you," his son said. "Old fart's too tight, even on Thanksgiving."

Cletus was much bigger than his father, broad-shouldered and barrel-chested. Now, though, too much brandy and too little work had done their damage. His jowls sank to the neck of his dirty T-shirt and the T-shirt barely covered his belly.

"None of your business where I got this drink," George said. "Ain't for you anyhow."

"Why'nt you bring home more'n one bottle, dumbass?" Cletus said, pointing at an almost empty fifth of brandy lodged between the turkey platter and a bowl of cranberry sauce. "That there's all's in the whole goddam house."

"'S matter with you then, ya lazy turd? Get off your fat can and—"

It was the kind of drunken jabber that could, and very often did, turn violent. But now George broke it off because the football game was about to start. He reached into the front pocket of his work shirt and pulled out a crumpled dollar bill. "Get your stakes on the table," he said.

Betting on a game was the only family ritual the Brauns had on holidays. Other than that, they didn't celebrate them, not even Christmas—unless buying a carton of Camels marked "Holiday Greetings" made for a celebration. Today they were having turkey dinner only because, early that morning, they'd found a box of food on the back doorstep. Where it came from, they had no idea.

Cletus had given the box a kick and said, "Pro'ly some goddam church in town thinks we need the charity. Feel like going in there and telling 'em—"

But he didn't go anywhere and his wife was the only person he told anything. "Nice to have sump'n on the table besides Dinty Moore's," he said to her now. "Or the rest of your crappy cooking."

From the kitchen counter, where she stood drinking brandy and cutting a pumpkin pie, Frances told him what he could do to himself.

She was a little woman, with brown hair and faded brown eyes. A purple bruise seeped across the knuckles of her right hand, put there that morning when she'd beaten her son with fist and firewood.

"Somebody turn the goddam radio on," George said. "And you, France-ass, ante up."

Frances was reaching into her apron pocket when Cletus yelled, "What the—?"

Naomi and Harold stood in front of the couch. Naomi held a shotgun.

The first blast slammed Cletus into the refrigerator. The second blew away George's head.

Frances stood frozen to the grey linoleum while Naomi reloaded. When she was done, she put the shotgun to her mother's breast and pulled the trigger.

What a wünderkind you were, Naomi. Smart and lucky, too.

Which is also what Sheriff Jackson thought.

I picked up Lowell Whalen's notebook and reread what his friend the sheriff had concluded about the Braun murders. "Sometime Thanksgiving afternoon," Whalen wrote, "one of the Braun children killed their parents and grandfather. Jackson says it was probably Naomi. Harold seems to lack the necessary physical and mental ability.

"Since only four empty shells were found, including one in the yard, Jackson thinks a single gun killed all three Brauns and the dog. The weapon was probably the 12-gauge side-by-side missing from the house. The shells had no fingerprints on them.

"All three murders occurred within a very short period of time, though their order is hard to determine. Jackson presumes the men were killed first, then the woman. The dog, which was no doubt barking its head off, was probably killed as an afterthought.

"The kitchen was pretty much awash in blood, but no footprints were found. 'Nothing to that,' Jackson says. 'The kids just didn't happen to walk through the blood. There'd be some on the shooter's clothes, though.

"Only the family's fingerprints were found inside the house. Whoever committed these murders was very careful, very instinctive. And very lucky.

"As to the careful part, Jackson figures the murders had been planned for a long time—planned for deer hunting season, when no one would pay attention to gunshots; planned for Thanksgiving, when there'd be few people around, few potential witnesses. A hideout had been carefully chosen, a new wardrobe gathered and stashed. A dumping spot for the shotgun had been scouted, an escape route planned, a cover story concocted.

"As for luck, first there was the weather—no snow had fallen yet but it was very cold out, the ground all but frozen. Secondly, nobody dropped by the Braun place, as country people might, to say Happy Thanksgiving. It was even lucky that George Braun must've mentioned the three Indians he saw in the bar."

I set Lowell Whalen's notebook aside, to pick up his daughter's interview with Naomi Braun. I'd lied to Kit when I said I'd never seen it before. I certainly had, any number of times over the past forty years. Again and again I'd read her description of Naomi: "A fidgety, ferret-faced girl with greasy hair and dirty fingernails . . . Her sly, hooded eyes cannot meet yours . . . She has poor grammar and a rudimentary vocabulary."

Kit was proud that the Milwaukee papers had picked up the interview—though all she'd really done was give her impressions of Naomi: "Secretive even when it isn't in her best interest . . . Perhaps a low IQ prevents . . ."

The interview mentioned Naomi's low IQ several times but carried very little about the murder, and most of that dead wrong. But what does journalistic integrity matter when Dad's the past president of the Publishers Association?

Sheriff Jackson, on the other hand, was right about quite a few things. Hal and Naomi—but I don't need to pretend anymore—Hal and I did stay in a remote cabin those three weeks. And, yes, I'd had it scoped out for months. It belonged to some Chicago people who didn't use it much but kept it well stocked anyway.

We drove most of the way there in the old Plymouth George had come up from Illinois in and left to disintegrate in the barn when he decided to stay. Hal had brought it back to life. The poor guy couldn't read or write, even talk really. But, oh my, was he ever good with machinery.

He was strong, too. We were both strong, outdoorsy farm kids who'd long since learned how to use a gun, drive a tractor. It didn't take much for us to push the Plymouth into Lake Downer, just like

I'd planned. Later, the shotgun went in, too.

But I have to admit that's pretty much where smart ends and lucky begins. I never have understood why no one found us. Matter of fact, no one came looking or even came around. Except the very first weekend, when I spotted a man prowling the woods not far from the cabin. A deer hunter, probably. I used my last shotgun shell on him and was lucky there, too. Not only did I miss, but he never came back.

When we'd eaten all the food in the cabin and burned the kerosene, we went into town. I told the story of the three Indians and stuck to it. Hal never said anything at all. Not until the day he died.

Why did I choose Thanksgiving? Not necessarily for the reasons the sheriff thought. Part of it was because that morning Frances had beaten Hal again. She was always a lot quicker with her fists than Cletus or George. They had other weapons. Mostly, I did it because when my dog tried to protect Hal, Cletus shot the poor thing dead.

The dog was called Stop, the word Hal had painted on the doghouse instead of Spot. I hated what Cletus and George always did to Stop. It was no different than what they did to me but George also poisoned Stop's pups. The first two or three litters, anyway. Then he took to drowning them, one at a time.

George drowned a litter the same night he did my baby.
***

It's been six days since I slipped the poison into Kit Whalen's coffee. I'm on my screen porch, grading papers—miserably written, as usual—and watching the neighbors drift in and out of Jerry's house.

They're offering their condolences because though steel beams aren't as efficient as a shotgun, they do get the job done. Yesterday afternoon, while Jerry was in Oshkosh, his wife met with a fatal "accident" at his studio. One of his big metal sculptures fell on her.

And now—though, of course, he doesn't know it yet—now Jerry and I will be together again, after all these years.

The End

SOMEONE'S IN THE KITCHEN

Strange as it seems, politicians don't get murdered very often. Maybe that's why people still like to hear me tell about State Senator James R. Rowse being killed at that cooking contest. "There he lay," I always start off. "On the kitchen floor in front of the ice box, mouth full of Cornish pasty and arsenic."

Then, of course, I always have to stop and explain why a small town schoolteacher like me was there when it happened. And that involves a little history lesson, which goes like this—Back in the forties and fifties, every church and lodge and rural township in southwest Wisconsin held a pasty supper at least once a year. What made this particular year's Willow Township supper unique was that it included a pasty-cooking contest. They claimed they were doing it as part of the state's centennial celebration. But I think the real reason was that all the county fairs were over by then and plenty of women were still looking for a blue ribbon.

I went to the contest alone because my husband took our little girl to the movies that night. Some cowboy show, I expect, which Lyle used for an excuse not to endure another pasty supper. But I had to attend. I taught Home Economics at the high school in town. Such events may not have been mentioned in my contract, but, believe me, they were part of my job, even when the contest didn't feature any of my students.

Willow Township Hall's gone now. But it stood three miles out the County blacktop and then another three over a gravel road that wound and dove and rose through the hills, past farm houses and hip-roofed barns and fields full of corn and cattle. 'Til finally a crude wooden sign announced: WILLOW TOWNSHIP PASTY CONTEST AND SUPER, FRI OCT. 9 1948. COME ON! COME

49

ALL! The hall itself was another half mile down a dirt lane, in a stand of willows by Oscar Creek.

It was a little after three in the afternoon, already looking like rain, when I pulled into the field next to the township's limestone hall. The field was already filled with cars and trucks—Fords and Nashes and GMCs, along with Tally Bligh's DeSoto and Ellie Vivian's battered LaSalle coupe. There was a big black Buick, too, which I figured must belong to Senator James R. Rowse. He'd be judging the contest.

I was surprised to see so many people that early. The threat of rain must've pulled the men off their combines and away to the contest with their wives. A dozen families milled around the yard, shaking the senator's hand and waiting for someone to open up the locked hall.

I remember wondering how the contest organizers had managed to get Senator Rowse there. Sure, he lived in the township, a sort of gentleman farmer who raised horses and had a small lead mine on his property. But he wasn't running for reelection and since when did Jimmy R do anything without a political motive?

Early that summer, after four terms in the state legislature, the senator suddenly announced he wouldn't be on the November ballot. Maybe he thought he'd go down with Truman—he was a Democrat in a traditionally Republican district—or maybe, at forty-nine, he was already tired of politics. Too bad, people said. Jimmy R made a good senator. Did right by farmers and main street, too. He'd fought the smart city slickers from Milwaukee to a standstill over road money, even got some abandoned lead mines started up again.

Still, whatever his future plans might've been, old habits die hard. There in the yard, he was working the little crowd with every bit of his glad-hand charm. And they were eating it up as usual.

The senator wasn't much to look at—a tall, skinny man with hooded hazel eyes and a balding head. His smile was as crooked as his teeth, but there was something about Jimmy R. What people call charisma nowadays, I guess. Anyway, he could sure make you feel special.

Like when he strode up to me. "France Johnson, isn't it?" he said, wringing my hand. "Well, Mrs. Johnson, let me tell you that if any of these pasties belong to your pupils, I can't wait to dig in."

We'd only met once before, but here he was calling me by name and offering just the right compliment. I knew it was an old politician's trick, but when he gave me that crooked smile I couldn't help thinking what a handsome man Jimmy R really was.

Presently, a sleek yellow Cadillac glided up to the hall's front door and out stepped the township chairman's wife holding the hall key. Her name was Norma Morse and she was surely the most beautiful woman in Willow Township.

"Sorry I'm late," she said to the crowd as she opened the door.

"You're sorry all right," someone said and someone else laughed.

Obviously, what Norma gained in looks she lost in popularity.

Norma and Jack Morse couldn't even be called gentlemen farmers; they just lived out in the country. Nowadays, of course, lots of people do, but back then it was kind of unusual. Jack Morse owned a construction company and didn't keep so much as a saddle horse. Nevertheless, money talks; he'd been elected township chairman.

Until then, Norma, a city girl from Madison, never made much effort to fit in with her neighbors. She preferred a fast little clique at the local country club. Recently, though, with her husband being the new chairman and she being no fool, Norma helped him make some renovations in the hall, then organized this pasty supper and contest to show them off. Even more astonishingly, she had the sense to put Ellie Vivian in charge. Seventy-year old Mrs. Vivian's late husband had been township chairman for three decades.

Putting locks on the hall doors, though, wasn't viewed as the most neighborly of gestures. Most of the township felt like Mrs. Vivian when she said, "Trusting soul, aincha?" as Norma let us in the kitchen door.

The kitchen, renovated or not, would never be called a Home Economics teacher's model of efficiency. But I could see that the Morses had done more than put in locks. True, an ice box did for refrigeration, but the high-backed sink had running water and the cupboards bore a fresh coat of white paint. New red oil cloth stretched across the counters and long, center table. Even the ancient cook-stove looked polished and serviceable.

When I asked Ellie Vivian how I could help, she said, "First off, Mrs. Johnson, you can get out the other one of these things." She grunted a little as she pulled a big white coffee pot down from the cupboard.

I suspected her arthritis was bothering her, though Mrs. Vivian wouldn't be one to complain. She was the kind of energetic little woman who earned every wrinkle in her face and every sinew in her arms. She'd spent a lifetime plowing fields, milking cows, keeping house, raising children—chickens, pigs, and horses, too. This in a climate where, summer to winter, temperatures could range 115 degrees and in a time before telephones or electric lights or gas-driven tractors. Even after her husband died and she quit farming, Mrs. Vivian still put in a full garden, which—to her daughters' horror—she tilled with a wheeled hand-plow, by herself.

Energetic, of course, doesn't always mean neat. This day, Mrs. Vivian wore a wrinkled green dress and stained butcher's apron, its deep pockets bulging with all the things other women kept in a purse. Her thick white hair was pulled into a barely controlled bun. The eyes behind her rimless glasses, though, were the calm brown of a woodland pond.

When we had the pots on the stove, she said, "You got good handwriting, Mrs. Johnson. Why don't you write the entrants' names down? Then give 'em these little flags with numbers on to stick in their pasties."

She handed me a fistful of the numbered flags, then went to scrub what she called the zinc. "Norma Morse shoulda done this," she said as she reached under the sink for a box of Gold Dust cleanser. "But she's so lazy she even hires somebody to clean her house."

I pulled up a spindly wooden chair and sat down at the center table. In ten minutes, I'd checked in four contestants; four delicious-looking pasties lined the counter.

After the contestants were finished in the kitchen, they went into the main room to join their families for the musical program that Norma Morse had also arranged. Darleen Arndt, local girl and music major at the University, was already at the piano playing from a pair of thick books marked Mozart and Mendelssohn. A fair-haired young man—I thought he looked a little brighter than Dar's usual taste in boyfriends—turned the pages.

I'd not known the first four contestants well, but the next one I did. She was Maxine Kitto and I was glad to see her out and about. The year before, Maxine's oldest son had been killed in a mining accident. The poor boy survived whatever awful places the Marines had sent him during the War, only to die less than seven miles from home.

Over night, Maxine became an old woman. Her brown eyes turned muddy and her curly dark hair went lank and grey. She stopped going out, even to church. The only reason anyone in town knew she was still alive was that, after her husband left the house in the morning, she turned on the phonograph as loud as it would go. For the next six hours, Verdi and Puccini blasted through the neighborhood. Until one morning three months back. The music suddenly stopped. Maxine came out of the house, swept the porch, and when that was done, went grocery shopping. People said she was herself again.

I wondered, though. Maxine's son had a dreadful death—he'd suffocated in a mine cave-in. Could I ever find a way to get over it if something like that happened to my child?

But it was a smiling Maxine who stood before me now. "You don't need bother with the rest of 'em. This here's the winner," she said, sliding the flag numbered Five into the crust of her pasty.

"Better just take it on home, Max," said the little red-haired woman behind her. "You couldn't win if you was the only one in the contest."

Maxine turned and pointed to the redhead's newspaper-wrapped pasty. "That a pasty or your garbage, Doris? Not's anybody'd know the difference."

Maxine and the redhead—Mrs. Vivian's married daughter, Doris Penhollow—had been talking to each other like this since they were six. That's when Maxine's mother died and her father disappeared into the bottle. Ellie Vivian had taken Maxine home—you could do that in those days, before the social workers started sticking their noses in—and raised her like her own.

Best friends and all but sisters for forty years, Doris and Maxine stood up at each other's weddings, were godmother to each other's children. Not surprisingly, it was Doris who, that July morning, turned off the Puccini, handed Maxine a broom, then drove her down to the A&P.

Doris was as full of verve as her mother, one of those people who truly seem to have energy shooting out of every pore. She'd raised four children, kept the books at her husband's bottling plant, and when all but one of the kids were out of the house, she became

53

an antique dealer. A prosperous one, too. She'd hit a farm auction, buy a walnut bedstead for a couple of dollars, then sell it to Chicago tourists for twenty. She once offered me a very nice sum for my Gone With the Wind lamp. But I figured if it was worth that much to Doris Penhallow, it was sure worth that much to me.

"Bout time you got here," Mrs. Vivian said.

"It's started to rain," her daughter said, waving toward the window above the sink. "And you know Max can barely drive inside the lines on the best of days."

"At least I don't use speed tickets for wallpaper," Maxine fired back.

Mrs. Vivian shook her head. "You two need something to do 'sides rip on each other," she said. "Start making the coffee, Maxine. And you, Doris, start cutting them pasties."

Grinning broadly, the women hopped to it.

But I didn't trust Doris Penhallow with other people's entries. Not after the 1944 County Fair when she'd "accidentally" knocked a rival's angel food cake onto the judging tent's dirt floor. And then stepped in it. "I stumbled," she claimed. "Ma always did say I was clumsy as a ox on ice." When her cake didn't take a ribbon after all, Doris consoled herself by winning the jitterbug contest.

"Somebody needs to set out the cups and plates," I said. "Maybe you could do that, Doris."

And she did, with such energy I thought she'd break half the set.

The next entrant was Tally Bligh. "Howya doing, France?" she said. "Missed you at bridge club the other night."

Tally wore a cream-colored Vera Maxwell-style suit that set off her dark hair. She was just about the best dressed woman in the county, but the really amazing thing about her clothes was that she made them. I was a pretty good teacher of sewing—if I do say so— but I've never claimed to be much of a seamstress myself. Oh, I could keep my daughter in skirts and shorts and me in house dresses. But never a suit like the one Tally had on. Nor, I have to admit, could I wear it with anything like Tally Bligh's style. She looked like a New York model, if not as tall—or, my husband pleased me by pointing out, as pretty.

As Tally added pasty Six to the ones already on the counter, Doris said, "Hope we can trust you not to try and poison Jimmy R even if he's not running again."

"Criminey, Doris," her mother said from the sink. "What's got into you?"

Certainly nothing new. Doris Penhallow went for the unprotected throat every time. In this case it was because Tally's husband had lost the last election to Senator Rowse by a landslide that completely buried any further political ambition.

But Tally was still a good political wife. With her warmest smile, she said, "Jimmy R's probably got a stomach of cast iron. Have to, after all the fund raisers he's been at. Democrats can't cook any better'n they can run the country."

It was a good line and Tally had the sense to exit on it.

"She can laugh now," Doris said. "But election time two years ago, she didn't think there was anything funny about Jimmy R, did she? And for sure not when he got through paying her husband back for daring run against him."

Maybe it was just coincidence, but the health department had begun seemingly endless inspections of Les Bligh's stock—for TB, for brucellosis, for hoof-and-mouth disease. And there'd been all kinds of trouble over some mortgaged cattle Les was alleged to have sold.

"A Republican woulda done the same," Maxine said from the stove where she'd started making coffee. "There's just no difference in the parties. That's why I'm gonna vote Progressive."

I was spared further political commentary by Norma Morse, who swept into the kitchen saying, "Didn't Tally stay to help? Guess she's worried about getting that pretty suit all full of pasty."

Norma didn't dress as well as Tally Bligh. She didn't need to. As I said, Norma was beautiful, even at forty and with her looks starting to fade. Like her blonde hair would've, too, without those biweekly visits to Bettsy's Beauty Parlor.

But no amount of bleach could hide the fact that Norma looked drawn. Had for quite a while, when I thought about it. Maybe the rumors were true—maybe her husband's construction company wasn't doing very well. In spite of the big postwar building boom, you saw more of Dan Roberts' signs around now and everyone knew Lance Trevalyan put in the low bid for blacktopping the county roads.

From behind her back, Norma produced a fat pasty. "Here's something that may surprise you," she said.

As a matter of fact, it did. By her own admission, Norma was no cook. But even more surprising was her offer to help in the kitchen. Seizing what was surely a rare moment, Mrs. Vivian promptly told her she could haul the tins of sugar and salt and cocoa out of their storage place under the counter. Norma obeyed promptly, and with surprising good grace.

Everyone was busy fetching and pouring and mixing when I went to tell Senator Rowse he could begin judging the pasties any time. I should've known it wouldn't be any time soon. Jimmy R had to show off first.

I stood by the kitchen door as the senator stepped to the front of the hall and launched into a little speech explaining how our part of the state was one of America's real melting pots: Cornish, German, Irish, Sicilian, Welsh, Norwegian. But, he said, at the table everyone was Cornish—a Cousin Jack. In southwest Wisconsin, pasty and saffron bread were as common as hamburgers and ice cream. And, therefore, everyone was an expert on how a pasty ought to be made.

"As I know all too well, dear friends," he said. "I also know a politician can't really afford to judge a cooking contest. So I guess you could say I'm celebrating my retirement by being here today."

He paused to give the crowd a chance to moan its sorrow that he'd no longer be their dear friend in Madison.

"I'll miss you, too," he said. "And since this will be one of my last talks, I'll make it one to remember by keeping it short."

Of course, he didn't. He explained at quite some length how the Marshall Plan was a good thing and school consolidation was a bad thing and we should for sure vote Democratic in November. Finally, he recalled where he was and launched into a history of the pasty.

"Pasties, my dear friends," the senator said, "were eaten as far back as the Middle Ages but they only came to Wisconsin in the 1840's, brought by Cornish miners. On a cold Wisconsin morning, a Cousin Jack would stick one of those portable pies down his shirt to keep both him and it warm. Then come dinnertime he'd put it on his shovel and reheat it over a miner's candle."

Everyone in the room had known all this by the time they were ten, but they cheered anyway. Jimmy R could always get his audience involved.

"In the bad old days over there in Cornwall, some pretty

disgusting things went in the pasties," he said with a grin. "Entrails and such."

"Yuk, blah," went the crowd.

"And you still never know what you might get from the Cousins up in northern Michigan."

Laughter from the crowd.

"But a pure pasty—a Wisconsin pasty—"

"Yay," went the crowd.

"Is onion and potato and round steak and that's all."

Now a few of the women cast nervous glances at each other. A recipe wasn't what you wanted to hear from a judge, especially if your pasty included turnip or carrots or rutabaga.

Perhaps Senator Rowse noticed the looks. Or perhaps, old pol that he was, he naturally sought compromise. "On the other hand," he said, "my dear old ma always claimed no two Cornishwomen would ever agree on what went in a pasty."

Nods from the crowd.

"So, dear friends—" He paused for effect, then finished with his best senatorial flourish. "As usual, the proof's in the pasty."

"Yay," went the crowd.

Yuk, I thought. I hadn't voted for Jimmy R and never would. I didn't doubt he was honest. Where money was concerned, anyway. And I knew his road initiatives had brought prosperity to the district. What I couldn't tolerate was his philandering.

My husband claimed the stories about Jimmy were just bridge-table gossip, but I knew better. Only the previous spring, one of my students had suddenly burst into tears in the middle of sewing class. When I asked if she wanted to talk, she said her folks were getting a divorce, all because of Senator Rowse.

Seems that a few weeks before, her mother told everyone she was going to visit a sick relative in Indiana. But that same weekend, Norma and Jack Morse saw her at the Palmer House in Chicago. She was arm in arm with Jimmy R.

As it turned out, the girl's parents hadn't divorced. Instead, the whole family moved to Sheboygan. And when I asked Norma Morse if the story was true, she said it had all come right in the end, so what did it matter? Besides, Norma said, if Madeleine Rowse could live with him, the district sure could.

I was left to wonder how many state road contracts Morse

Construction would be getting.

When the applause finally died down, Jimmy came into the kitchen. Not quite finished with his antics, he soon had us singing "Someone's in the Kitchen with Dinah" while he belted out the chorus in a pretty fair baritone. Of course, the crowd loved it. This time they took a very long time to stop clapping.

Finally, he shooed us into the hall's main room. "Lovely, ladies, just lovely," he said. "We should go on Amateur Hour for sure."

My last sight of James R. Rowse alive was as he was setting a plate of pasty on the center table next to his Camels and cup of hot chocolate.

"It's my show now," he said in that rich baritone. Then he flung out his arms like a vaudeville performer leaving the stage.

As Mrs. Vivian and I took chairs in the back of the hall, she said, "Rain's really starting to come down. Knew it'd get bad. Durn arthritis makes me feel like Joe Lewis's punching bag."

Eight pasties can be judged in well under half an hour, but nearly forty-five minutes went by with the senator still at it. The crowd was getting restless even though Dar had sensibly switched from Mozart to Tin Pan Alley.

"He's sure taking his sweet time in there," Mrs. Vivian said. "I better go find out what the problem is."

She started to get up, but I could see she was in pain. I went instead.

"Having a hard time choosing, Senator?" I said as I closed the kitchen door behind me. "Sometimes it's really difficult. I know when I have to judge . . ."

My voice trailed off. I was talking to an empty kitchen.

The pasties were still there, in a neat line on the counter next to the stacked dishes. The pots of coffee and hot chocolate were on the stove. At one end of the center table sat a plate of partially eaten pasty, a fork, the senator's cigarettes and ashtray. Everything was just as we'd left it.

The senator, though, was nowhere to be seen.

His chair was pushed back from the table, and so, thinking he'd gone out to his car—forgotten matches could send a heavy smoker like Jimmy R into the worst of downpours—I started toward the back door. But, no, it was hooked shut.

I went around the center table. Senator Rowse lay between the table and the ice box.

He was dead. I knew that right away. And I also knew he'd died in agony. His knees were pressed to his chest, his face contorted with pain. He was covered in vomit.

At first, all I could do was stand over his crumpled body, unable to form a prayer for his soul, almost unable to form any thought at all.

Then Mrs. Vivian came into the kitchen. "What's taking so long out here?"

Still shocked dumb, I waved a hand in the direction of the senator.

When she saw him, Mrs. Vivian's mouth opened, closed, opened. "How are the mighty fallen," she said finally.

That broke the spell and I mumbled my prayer.

Composed now, Mrs. Vivian said, "Lookit all that puke, will ya."

Brown vomit splattered the floor between table and ice box, then trailed along to the sink, which also had some in it.

"Must be food poisoning took him," Mrs. Vivian said.

My first thought was oh please, not food poisoning. Not with half Willow Township on the other side of the door. I didn't think anyone else had eaten or drunk anything yet. But if they had . . . Thank God Mrs. Vivian was a stouthearted farm woman who wouldn't panic.

To give myself some time to think, I went and put the hook on the door to the main room. Then I looked at the partially eaten pasty on the table and said, "I think he only had a few bites."

But Senator Rowse had vomited up what pasty he'd eaten. Some of the hot chocolate he'd drunk and a few undigested hunks of meat and crust and potato spilled down his white shirt and over his loosened tie. The rest of what he'd brought up was brown and blood-streaked.

One thing a Home Economics teacher knows about is household danger, about lye and rubbing alcohol and DDT. And certainly about food poisoning. So, unless the senator had been highly allergic to something, I was sure this couldn't be ordinary food poisoning or even botulism.

"They both take hours to kill," I said. "Or, sometimes, even to show up. And for certain to make someone as sick as this."

"That so?" Mrs. Vivian said, glancing doubtfully from me to the senator to the pasty on the table. "Well, maybe he got it someplace else. Like at home. Madeleine Rowse ain't no great shakes as a cook."

"He said he hadn't eaten all day."

"So's he could give the contest his all, I s'pose," Mrs. Vivian said and shook her head.

By then, I was thinking hard. Maybe the senator strangled on his own vomit. Or maybe he'd aspirated some foreign object. But that happened mostly to drunks and, as far as I could tell, Jimmy R had been stone sober.

"Could be a heart attack," Mrs. Vivian said. "I heard it was on account of his heart he decided not to run again."

I'd heard so, too, but I didn't think that's what killed him. My father died of a heart attack and there'd been no vomiting. But this was like something else I'd seen—a long time ago, before Pop died, before we moved to town.

One of the hired men had killed himself, dying in such agony that Pop said, "If he'da just asked, I'da give him my shotgun."

Instead, the man drank arsenic.

His death taught me that arsenic may be tasteless and odorless but it causes the very worst kind of stomach pain. Nor is the pain made any better by the ceaseless vomiting that follows.

I went to the sink and yanked open the door to the cabinet beneath. There, lodged with the dish soap and the scrub brushes and the cleanser was an open can of Atlas 60 weed-killer. It probably contained enough arsenic to kill everyone in the building. Twice over.

"We need to call the sheriff," I told Mrs. Vivian.

"The sheriff?" she said. "He's pro'ly the other side of the county, joy-riding in his fancy new patrol car. What we need's an undertaker."

"The senator's been murdered."

Mrs. Vivian shoved her hands into the big pockets of her apron. "You ain't a doctor," she said.

"No," I said. "But I know he's been poisoned."

After taking another look at the senator's body, Mrs. Vivian shook her head and sighed. "McGuire's is pro'ly the closest phone. But you better go. My eyes ain't up to four miles in the rain and it getting dark, too."

I said we should both stay. "If anybody comes in and finds out the senator's dead, we'll have a panic on our hands. People'll be all over the . . . the scene of the crime, destroying evidence and such."

"So what's us two gonna do? Set up Big Bertha in here, blow the curious away?"

"I'll take care of it," I said, then slipped through the door to tell the crowd that Senator Rowse was taking longer than planned. They shifted in the folding chairs, grumbling or laughing according to their natures.

To Dar, I whispered, "Get them singing. Hymns, The Old Gray Mare, Mairsy Doats. Anything, so long as they're amused."

To Dar's boyfriend, I said, "Come with me."

The young man turned out to be as sensible as I'd hoped. He barely blinked when I told him Senator Rowse was dead, nodded solemnly as I gave him directions to McGuire's. His driving might've been another matter, if the jack rabbit start he gave our Ford was any indication.

When I'd seen him down the lane, I turned from the kitchen window. "It's really coming down out—Oh my God, don't do that."

Mrs. Vivian was clearing off the center table. She'd already pushed the senator's chair back to the table and now had his ashtray in her hand, ready to dump it in the garbage pail. I snatched it away and put it back on the table, next to his cigarettes and the plate of pasty.

"Just keeping busy," Mrs. Vivian said in a defensive tone.

That's when it occurred to me that this stout farm woman might be as unhinged by the situation as I was. "I'm sorry," I said. "It's just that a person doesn't often stumble across a murdered senator."

"You better be careful, calling this murder when you ain't got a scrap of cause."

Didn't I? There were any number of people who wouldn't mind seeing the senator dead. And some of them had just walked through this very kitchen.

Tally Bligh, for instance, might want to end her husband's difficulties with the state authorities. Norma Morse might be unhappy that no state road jobs had paid for the Morses' silence after all. And Maxine Kitto had an even better reason. The accident that killed her son happened at the Rowse lead mine.

Then there were the rumors about Jimmy R and Doris Penhallow—that she'd gone ahead and filed for divorce but when the star dust settled he was still married to Madeleine.

"I'll have the bastard's nuts," Doris told everyone in the Blue

Goose and the Green Lantern and half a dozen other taverns spread over three counties.

And those were just the people I knew about. At the legislature in Madison, Jimmy R had probably made enemies from here in the Lead Region all the way up to the North Woods.

I suppose anybody else would have left it right there, for the sheriff to pursue. But my husband always said I was constitutionally incapable of passing up a puzzle. Not a jigsaw, not the crossword in the paper, not even an unnecessary double finesse at bridge. In other words, I couldn't help but try and figure out who killed Senator James R. Rowse.

And Mrs. Vivian seemed just as engrossed. While I leaned against the counter thinking about people and their motives, she paced the kitchen from end to end and back again. Her old eyes seemed to study every detail. Sometimes she'd glance across the center table at Senator Rowse and nod her head.

Presently, she jabbed a finger toward the cut pasty on the table, the one he'd begun with. "Whose is that? It ain't got a number."

I looked at the pasties still on the counter. Number Seven was missing.

"That's Tally Bligh's number," Mrs. Vivian said. "And it's the same number as on that flag over there by the corpse."

The little flag, which I hadn't noticed before, lay by the senator's elbow, in a puddle of brown vomit.

Mrs. Vivian shook her head. "Always knew Tally held political grudges," she said. "But I never figured her for no killer."

Nor had I. I went back to the cut pasty on the table. Something about it seemed wrong. Over the years I'd eaten enough of Tally Bligh's pasties to know that the crescent in its crust wasn't her work. The pasty's shape was wrong, too. With a clean spoon, I gently peeled back a bit of crust.

"Hey, there," Mrs. Vivian said. "Who's destroying evidence now?"

"I don't think this is Tally's pasty. She's a steak-potatoes-onion woman. So Flag Seven can't go with this pasty. It's got rutabaga in it."

Mrs. Vivian came for a look. "So it does. What's that stuff all over the top?"

In my concern with the ingredients and the numbers, it hadn't registered that the pasty was sprinkled with something that looked like sugar. I dipped a finger in it and darn near took a taste before I realized what I was doing. The stuff might be weed-killer.

I rushed to the sink and washed my hands. "Maybe I better stop playing Nora Charles and just wait for the sheriff."

If he ever got there. Not all the roads were paved and in heavy rain even new patrol cars could get stuck. Leaning across the sink's high back and moving a cup off the window ledge behind it, I pressed my face against the window. It was so dark I could barely see to the outhouse, and raining harder than ever.

Out in the other room, Dar had done as I asked and kept the crowd well entertained. But now someone was knocking at the kitchen door.

In a firm voice, Mrs. Vivian said, "Go on. He ain't finished."

The knocking stopped and she said, "I could use a cup of coffee. How 'bout you?"

She poured coffee from one of the big white pots one the stove.

I took a cup and went to inspect the line of pasties on the counter. About half were sprinkled with the same pale powder as on the pasty Senator Rowse had tasted.

"Poison, huh?" Mrs. Vivian said when she joined me.

"Looks like it. And it looks like whoever killed the senator wanted to make sure they got the job done."

Or maybe not. Arsenic is lethal, no question of that. But the light dusting on these pasties just wouldn't do the trick. The same was true of the one Jimmy R had sampled.

That's when it occurred to me something very strange was going on. Jimmy had eaten a little of the pasty on the table, that was clear. But it hadn't killed him. Nor, I felt sure, had the weed-killer sprinkled on top of it.

The real poison must have come from some other source. Why, then, bother putting arsenic on top of this pasty? The obvious answer was so the blame would fall on Tally. Her pasty, her arsenic.

But maybe it didn't matter to the killer whose pasty Jimmy chose first. Maybe that was the reason for arsenic being sprinkled on the others, too. Its presence would make any owner seem guilty.

Again I looked at the line of pasties on the counter. Setting down my coffee, I touched each of their flags. They were in no particular order—number 6, then 3, 1, 5, and so forth. But the crystals were only on those closest to where Jimmy had sat; in other words, on the ones he would have reached for first.

What could all this mean?

Bamboozled and restless, I went back to the window. It was so dark now I not only had to lean across the sink and press my nose against the pane, I also had to put my hands around my face to see outside. Of course, there was nothing to see. I gave the window a hard rap.

"What was that?" Mrs. Vivian said. She sounded thoroughly alarmed.

"Just me," I told her. Then I told myself to calm down. And think.

I turned from the window, picked up my coffee cup, leaned back against the sink. To watch Mrs. Vivian pace the kitchen. And to think.

What if the sprinkled arsenic was just a ruse to confuse matters? But even if it was, the killer must have known it would only work for a little while. So again, why bother?

And something else. The seven pasties still on the counter all had flags. So if the pasty that Jimmy tasted, the one with rutabaga in it, wasn't Tally's, the killer must have switched flags.

"Whatcha thinking?" Mrs. Vivian asked.

"That the killer tried to muddy the . . . uh . . . crime scene by sprinkling around arsenic and, maybe, switching flags."

"I don't get it."

"Me neither. Especially the flags being switched."

"Let's have some more coffee," Mrs. Vivian said. "Maybe it'll help you see things clearer."

She reached for my cup. But by then I was hanging onto it like it was something out of those silly magazines my husband read—a time machine that would transport me back to the scene in the kitchen just before Senator Rowse came in—

Tally puts her pasty on the counter, then fends off Doris's nasty comment. She goes into the hall's main room. Norma comes into the kitchen.

I'm at the center table, with Doris putting out the supper dishes while Maxine deals with the pots on the stove. Norma gets out the sugar and cocoa tins. Later, she sets an ashtray on the table next to the dishes Mrs. Vivian has lain out for Senator Rowse. "Jimmy R'll need this," Norma says. "The man smokes like a chimney."

After that, I go to fetch him and, when he finishes his speech, he comes to the kitchen. We all sing.

No, only Mrs. Vivian, Maxine, Doris, and I sing. Norma left the kitchen when I went to get the senator. Now she's across the room, sitting with her husband.

Mrs. Vivian's voice returned me to the present. "More coffee?"

I glanced down at my cup. And did a double take. Whatever was in it didn't look like coffee. Hot chocolate, I thought. Or it had been. Now there was only some brown muck in the cup, along with a gob of white stuff that had separated out.

Arsenic, I was willing to bet. And more than willing to bet Senator Rowse had drunk enough to kill him.

I set the cup on the drain board and, pushing Mrs. Vivian away from the stove, pulled the lid off the pot of hot chocolate.

It looked all right. When I poured a little into a saucer, that looked all right, too.

"What you up to?" Mrs. Vivian said.

I pointed at the cup on the drain board. "I'm sure not going to sample it, but I'm positive there's arsenic in it."

"But I seen you drinking out of it."

I went and picked the cup up. "Not out of this one. I drank out of that one."

I waved at a cup sitting by the other dishes on the counter. The two cups looked alike. In fact, all the cups looked alike, heavy war surplus mugs marked U.S. Army Medical Department. But the one I meant was half full of coffee.

"This cup," I said, now meaning the one in my hand. "This is the one I picked up before. It was on the sill between the sink and the window."

Mrs. Vivian's gaze went from one cup to the other and back again.

"This is the senator's hot chocolate," I said. "But I can't remember who gave it to him."

Mrs. Vivian stirred more sugar into her coffee.

In that moment the puzzle came together.

"You killed Senator Rowse," I said.

Mrs. Vivian laughed.

"Doris, then. Or Maxine."

She stopped laughing.

"All three of you had plenty of opportunity to spike that cup of chocolate when you were in the kitchen by yourselves."

"So did Norma Morse," she said. "Or, for that matter, yourself."

"But Norma didn't have any real reason to kill the senator. And I, even less. You, on the other hand—you and Doris and Maxine—had Joe Kitto."

Joe Kitto, Maxine's son—Mrs. Vivian's all-but-grandson—had died in James Rowse's lead mine.

We stood staring at each other, until she sighed and said, "I s'pose that's what you'll tell the sheriff."

"I'll sure say Maxine had a motive."

Mrs. Vivian glanced at the door to the room where Doris and Maxine sat. She looked back at me, then at the door again. Her lips twisted. "The son of a bitch let Joe stay down that mine shaft, choking to death on poison gas. Said Joe was all right. Said after the vent quit, the other men seen him run out a drift. Said nobody could get killed in a mine of his. Said just go on home and wait."

She fished a handkerchief out of an apron pocket and swiped away a tear.

"We waited and waited. But Joe never come home and Jimmy Rowse never sent nobody down the mine to find him. Not till it was too late, anyhow."

"So Maxine—or maybe it was Doris—decided to get even by poisoning Rowse. And where better than at the cooking contest."

"Maxine didn't do nothing. Doris neither. It was Norma Morse that convinced the senator to judge the contest."

"Well, someone brought arsenic in here," I said. "Or maybe it was already here—in that open can of weed-killer under the sink."

Again, I summoned my mental picture of the scene in the kitchen. "When you got out the things to scrub the sink, you slipped the can into one of those big apron pockets. And while everybody was busy with her own chores, you set a place for the senator at the table. Knife, fork, spoon, and a nice cup of hot chocolate laced with weed-killer."

Mrs. Vivian took off her glasses and polished them with her handkerchief.

"But afterward you wondered where his cup went, didn't you? That's why you kept pacing the kitchen, looking everywhere. Well, he must've carried it over to the sink, maybe when he went to throw up. Anyway, he set it down on the window ledge, where it happened to be out of sight. Then I moved it off the ledge without even looking at it and later mistook it for my cup of coffee."

Mrs. Vivian put on her glasses and stuffed the handkerchief into an apron pocket.

"At some point—probably while I was out talking to Dar Anderson—you sprinkled weed-killer on the other pasties. A clever enough red herring, I guess. But what I don't understand is why you tried to pin the murder on Tally Bligh."

I glanced at the pasty Senator Rowse had sampled. At the yellowish pieces of rutabaga in it.

"That's it!" I said. "Tally Bligh doesn't put rutabaga in her pasty but Doris sure does."

Mrs. Vivian shoved both hands deep into her apron pockets.

"I think that when you came back into the kitchen just after I found the senator's body, you saw that he'd picked number Six—Doris's pasty—to begin on. A tough few minutes, even though I didn't notice the number on the flag. Then I went to talk to Dar Roberts and you could switch Doris's number for a different one."

Mrs. Vivian's face gave nothing away.

"You probably did it at the same time you sprinkled weed-killer on the other pasties. A clever enough red herring, I guess. But your arthritis slowed you down. You didn't have time to sprinkle the arsenic around and get the weed-killer back under the sink and exchange the two flags. You only had time to pull flag seven, go to the counter, switch Six for Seven. Then I was at the door and you were still holding flag Six. So you tossed it next to the body."

Mrs. Vivian dug her hands deeper into her apron pockets.

"But I don't think you were in this alone," I said. "Maxine was the one I saw with the pot of hot chocolate in her hand."

That was the wrong thing to say. Mrs. Vivian's hands shot out of the apron. With one hand she grabbed my belt and yanked me close. With the other she put a boning knife to my throat. "Doris always claimed you was too smart for your own good. Guess she was right."

The thin blade had drawn blood. When I felt it ooze down my neck, I decided I didn't care if she was an old lady or not. I smashed a fist down on her wrist. The knife flew out of her hand.

After that, I should've dealt with her pretty quickly. She was twice my age and I'd been a darn good athlete. Unfortunately, I forgot the obvious—I was no longer jump-center on my class basketball team at Milwaukee-Downer College but Ellie Vivian still plowed her garden.

Next thing I knew, she had me on the floor, on my belly with one arm pinned behind my back. Then she was astride me working the arm off its shoulder. I howled like an animal.

I also fought like one. She might've been stronger but I was heavier. Besides that, she was arthritic. I reached back with my free hand, grabbed her by the hair, and bucked and yanked and screamed until she fell off. Then I rolled on top of her and gave her a hard elbow to the solar plexus. Her breath rushed out. She let go my arm.

When the sheriff finally showed up, I had her hog-tied with my belt and two dish towels.

The following spring, Ellie Vivian—and Ellie Vivian alone—was tried and convicted of killing Senator James R. Rowse. Three years later, she died. Not, however, in the State Penitentiary for Women at Taycheedah. At seventy-one she was too old for prison.

Or so the governor said when he granted her clemency. Strange as it seems, politicians back then were even dumber than they are now.

The End

THE HEMINGWAY READER

I hesitated at first. Then Mr. A told me what he'd pay. It was enough to finish grad school.

He needed to do a favor for a friend but didn't want to give the job to anyone local. So he called me all the way from Chicago, said he'd heard my name around. Heard I used to lived in Wisconsin.

Do it, I told myself, and you'll have your PhD and be the Hemingway specialist at . . . Well, Berkeley wasn't altogether out of the question.

And while I was Up North, I could have a canoe adventure, too.

I'd just turned twenty-three that September and wasn't much of a canoeist—or an adventurer, either, no matter how much Hemingway I read. But I'd been in Scouting for a while as a kid, long enough to learn to do a J-stroke and to get off the lake when a hard wind came up.

Since Mr. A was sending me to the North Woods anyway, a canoe trip seemed like just the ticket. I needed escape. From L.A., of course, and riots and dead heroes—and Chris and rock 'n' roll and the war. I needed someplace that wasn't 1968.

"Know where I can rent a canoe for a couple days," I asked the bartender in a dark little tavern in northern Wisconsin.

He looked me up and down with the same doubting glower he'd given my driver's license when I ordered a beer. "Depends what you wanna do with it," he said.

I wanna shove it up your ass, I almost told him. But a glance at the men strung along the bar made me hold my tongue. No need to wise off around half a dozen guys who drank boilermakers at noon.

"Fishing trip," I said, touching my new mustache and grinning.

"Me and . . . um . . . you know, a friend."

The bartender's glower grew even darker, but one of his drinkers laughed. "Way to go." He raised his shot glass my direction.

I relaxed then. Nobody was going to give me guff about my long hair. Or why I wasn't in Nam.

"You could try Timberlodge," the bartender said, but more to his customers than me. "Lotsa fish over there, know what I mean?"

I didn't, but apparently everybody else did. They guffawed like the yokels in a John Wayne movie.

When they were done, the man who'd raised his glass said, "Up here fish means Fucking Illinois Shit Heads. You ain't from Chicago, are you?"

I told him not to insult me, which gained not only a laugh but some honest advice about where I could find a canoe.

"Schmidt's used to have fishing boats," said a little red haired guy. "But he's shut down, ain't he?"

A man in a buffalo shirt answered. "Had some kinda attack, Schmidt did. Right after their boy got killed in that hunting accident. Think the resort's still open, though. Don't know what they rent."

One or two more places were mentioned, then silence fell over the bar. Canoe rentals weren't exactly thick on the ground this late in the year. At Timberlodge, they did have a few, for a price only rich Chicagoans could handle. I figured I'd do better at Schmidt's.

Which took half the afternoon to find. It lay on one of the bigger lakes but in a back bay miles off the county highway through a wooded maze of gravel road and dirt lane.

The resort itself was pleasant enough, four little cabins set on an acre or two carved out of the pine forest. They were made of vertical half-logs freshly painted a dark red. Their screened porches faced the lake and the boat shed that jutted into it.

A larger cabin, also red but not so fresh-painted, stood back from the rest. By its drive, next to a black GMC, was a sign that read "Schmidt Cottages and Boat Rent. Closed For The Season."

A middle-aged woman came out of the house. She had faded blonde hair and wore an apron over her shirt and trousers.

"Sorry," she said when I rolled down the car window. "We ain't open. Maybe for fishing next spring. But there's already a waiting list."

I said I only wanted to rent a canoe.

Her eyes gave me a going over that made the bartender's seem like a love tribute. "How old are you?"

"Twenty-one." I reached for my billfold.

She waved away the driver's license. "We just got a few jon boats," she said. "No canoes."

In that case, I wanted to ask, what are the two items on the rack by your boat shed?

Following my gaze, then glancing back at the house, the woman said, "How long you need it for?"

"A couple days."

"That long?"

Willing to compromise, I said, "Tomorrow, then."

She looked at the house again as if she were seeking permission from someone inside. But there was no one at the picture window or, as far as I could see, on the screen porch either.

"The aluminum one's seven bucks," she said.

I knew aluminum canoes could be noisy, just what I didn't need. I said I'd take the other one.

"That'll be ten."

It was probably more than she usually got, maybe a lot more, but still cheaper than Timberlodge. I pulled a five and some singles out of my billfold.

"Seven'll be ok," the woman—I figured she was Mrs. Schmidt—said. "But we don't provide shuttles. You'll have to get back on your own."

"Not a problem," I said as I held out the seven dollars.

"Long as you understand that," she said, taking the money and shoving it into an apron pocket.

Mrs. Schmidt shot another glance at the house. There was someone on the screen porch. Her husband, probably.

He was the man I'd come to kill.

After my canoe trip.

I parked behind a cabin where it couldn't be seen from the lane. I'd stolen the car in Madison, almost two hundred miles away. Still, there was no use taking chances.

I went to help Mrs. Schmidt with the canoe, a 16-foot Old Town, by no means new. It was bigger than I'd have liked, but, short of a howling gale, I figured I could handle it.

We carried it to a sandy little beach nestled between a big willow tree and a patch of lily pads. I set to stowing my gear. By the time I finished, Mrs. Schmidt had brought a life-preserver and a paddle with the varnish peeling off.

"This should fit you," she said. And sure enough, when I measured it toe-top to chin-bottom, it did.

"Thanks," I said. "And don't worry. I'll take care of it all."

As I bent down to pull off my boots, Mrs. Schmidt said, "You sure got a mop of curly hair."

"My sister says I look like a poodle in desperate need of a groomer. You don't want to know what my dad says."

"Fathers can be awful hard on their kids, their boys." Mrs. Schmidt smiled a little. "I think your hair's just fine."

I thanked her again, tossed pad and paddles into the canoe. "Guess I'll be off now," I said.

"You'll be back tomorrow for sure?"

Oh shit, I thought. What's this? But when I looked at her, she still wore the little smile.

"Bring everything you need with you? You know, warm clothes? Rain gear?"

Pointing at my backpack already in the canoe, I said I'd be fine and, anyway, the forecast was for fair weather.

"Well," she said. "Up here, you never know what'll happen."

She helped me push the canoe into the water and held on while I climbed in.

The canoe rocked like crazy.

"Steady as you go," Mrs. Schmidt said.

The canoe righted itself and I began paddling. The knack of it came back quickly enough, so I was already a couple hundred yards into the lake by the time I turned to look back at shore.

A man had joined Mrs. Schmidt on the beach, to watch me through binoculars.

Of course, the lake was blue and the sun bright and the trees a glorious red and gold. Just like on every postcard in every store in every town north of Highway 8, I thought cynically. That Paradise Regained stereotype was the point for city-slickers like me. The old-time loggers knew northern Wisconsin better than that. "Hayward to Hurley to Hell," they described it.

For an hour or so, I stuck close to the shoreline so I could listen to the breeze soughing through the trees and watch Blue Herons standing one-legged in the shallows.

When I got tired of that, I paddled farther out and made myself a nice little berth in the bottom of the canoe. With the life-preserver for padding, I leaned against the seat and stretched my legs under the thwarts. My business with Art Schmidt wasn't till morning.

What would the canoe do without anyone in control? Would it drift along or go in a circle or stop dead? I didn't care. I just wanted to sleep in the sun for a while.

When I woke, the canoe was in a stump-clogged little cove, safely nestled against a fallen white birch. I paddled back into the lake and discovered that I could no longer see Schmidt's or any other sign of human habitation.

Back in the cove, I tossed the leader around the birch and slipped into the shallow water. When the canoe was ashore, I put on my boots and went into the forest.

The Scouts had taught me fairly well. The first thing I did was find a good spot to pitch camp. The only problem was, with all the cedars around, it smelled too much like gin.

Everything went easily. There was plenty of dry down wood in every size from tender to thigh-thick logs. True, the logs took some chopping, but even with only a hatchet I split them in no time.

I laid the wood in the teepee-style I'd been taught in Scouts, then lit it with one of the kitchen matches I kept in a metal Band-Aid box along with my cigarettes.

Fire blazing nicely, I spread out a ground sheet and my sleeping bag. The thing was an ugly khaki and probably left over from the Korean War. I laughed when the clerk at the army surplus store called it a mummy bag.

I'd brought The Hemingway Reader so I could reread "Big Two-Hearted River" by campfire. And eat canned beans and spaghetti fried up together, just like Nick Adams in the story. But by the time I finally had a pan over the fire, it was already dark. The fire didn't give off enough light and my flashlight was pretty dim.

I was beat anyway, so when I finished the beans and spaghetti—not too bad, really—I opened my canteen and dumped a little water into my mess kit, swished it around, and threw the rest on the fire. I used an army surplus trenching tool to bury the fire, smoked a cigarette, crawled into my mummy bag. I slept like the dead.

The next morning was clear but cold, so I put on heavy hunting socks and pulled my new red wool Pendleton shirt over the T-shirt and blue jeans I'd slept in. Then I got to work.

I took out my pistol, an Iver Johnson .22 Cadet. The model had become rather notorious in recent months, after Sirhan Sirhan used one to kill Bobby Kennedy. The only difference was that Sirhan had the short barreled version. That and the fact he got caught.

My gun had been stolen months before from a sporting goods store in Skokie, its serial numbers filed off, and was, Mr. A guaranteed me, untraceable. Not that anyone would ever find the thing once I got done with it. I poked eight .22 longs into its cylinder and stowed it in my backpack.

I put the canoe in the water, tossed in the backpack and my boots, paddled back to Schmidt's.

When I was still several hundred yards away, I could see a man watching through binoculars. By now, my boots were on and the .22 tucked under my shirt in the waistband of my jeans.

After I'd put in, Schmidt didn't even wait to ask if I was done with the canoe before he said, "Take your shit out and help me carry this thing back to the rack."

He shoved the binoculars into the case on his belt and, while I got out of the canoe, fished a battered pack of Camels from his shirt pocket. "My wife," he said, "told me you was a guy."

Before I could stop it, my hand went to my face.

The mustache was gone.

I hadn't planned to kill Schmidt out where the sound of a shot might carry across the lake. But now there didn't seem to be any choice. Neither masculine bravado nor feminine wiles would stave off his questions.

As Schmidt touched a match to his cigarette, I drew my pistol and fired.

I was lucky. The shot hit him in the throat and was enough to bring him down. I used the life-preserver to muffle the sound while I finished him off with five or six more bullets to his body and one behind his ear.

Later, I went into the house and tied up Mrs. Schmidt.

"Is he dead?" she asked.

I said he was.

"Thank you," she said in a strangled voice. "The bastard deserved it. After what he let happen to our son."

I told her I didn't want to know anything about it.

That silenced her for about a microsecond. "I wasn't going to let you have the canoe," she said. "Till I realized you were a girl. Like Tony told me he'd send. You don't think the sheriff'll figure it out, do you?"

I slapped a length of duct tape across her mouth. She could figure the rest out by herself.

That afternoon, I tossed the .22 into another lake and left the car on a street in Wausau. Then I caught a bus heading south.

I still have Schmidt's binoculars, by the way. And a PhD.

The End

ADDIO, MIA MADRE

One afternoon last May, I interrupted my secretary at her computer. "Time for a break, Dawn. Get yourself something to drink and come on in the office."

Dawn nodded at the screen. "Hey, Susan, you know Judge Poplawski wants this tomorrow morning."

"What I've got to tell you is more important," I said.

And it was. Because I'd found a way to save my law firm—and make both Dawn and me filthy, filthy rich.

In short, I had found Dawn's mother.

My name is Susan Llewellyn and for six years Dawn was my secretary and bookkeeper. My administrative assistant, she wanted me to say. As if my law firm were big enough to employ anyone with so lofty a title. On the other hand, Dawn had worked for me since she was in high school. So why should I care if she liked for her business cards to read: Llewellyn & Llewellyn, Attorneys at Law/Dawn Deborah von Stade, Administrative Assistant.

She liked her name, too, and the opera stars she built it out of. They were her role models, even if she couldn't sing a note. Maybe she needed them because she never had a mother. I mean a real mother, not that series of foster moms Milwaukee County social services stuck her with until she was eighteen.

I often wondered why Dawn never looked for her real mother. I know she didn't because she would have told me. Like she told me about the boys she went with or how she felt when she saw Puccini's Suor Angelica. But whenever the subject of her mother came up, she'd laugh it off with some crack like, "What if she wasn't Renee Fleming after all?"

Then, last winter, I found Dawn's mother.

The original Llewellyn & Llewellyn were my father and his younger brother. Then, just about the time I finished law school, Uncle Frank finally succeeded in drinking himself to death. So Daddy took me on. I'd been reluctant, of course. Pride, though, doesn't fill an appointment book and I knew very well that Smiling Jack Llewellyn never lacked for clients.

He's been dead for almost three years, but his office—my office now—hasn't changed much. Except for the oriental rug, which I added, the room has the same view of Lake Michigan, the same law book-lined walls and leather wing chairs, the same old-fashioned partners' desk. Daddy used to say that desk was big enough to play nine holes of golf on. A good thing, too, because under my proprietorship it teems with every office device known to 21st century technology—and, in its middle drawer, the snub nose .38 Chiefs Special my ex-husband claimed no desk was complete without.

I was at the desk when Dawn came in with coffee for me, Pepsi for herself. While I fussed with my briefcase, sorting and resorting its contents, she pulled one of the leather chairs over to the window and, sipping pop, gazed into the grey Milwaukee spring.

Finally, I set the briefcase on the floor, picked up my coffee, and said, "Hope you and Mike don't have plans for tonight. I've got a lot to tell you."

"We broke up. Tell me what?"

"Sorry about Mike," I said, though I didn't feel very sorry and wasn't so sure Dawn did either. The guy was a real jerk.

"Tell me what?"

I folded both hands around my cup. "You've met my friend Claudia, haven't you?"

Dawn heaved a dramatic sigh and said, "Why does it take lawyers so long to get to the point?"

"My friend Claudia?" I repeated.

"She the tall one with the salt and pepper hair and the million dollar suits?"

"These days, Claudia gets most of her clothes at—" I named one of the city's classier resale shops. The same one I buy at, though Claudia says designer labels never look quite right on stubby redheads.

"If she's that cheap," Dawn said, "what about the handmade

pumps? And the top donor's seat at the opera?"

"Ever notice how much you and Claudia look alike? Except for the hair, of course."

"And the shoes."

"What are you now? Twenty-three?"

"Pert'near twenty-four," Dawn said. "What's all this about?"

"I've known Claudia Pfeiffer since University School and at your age she could've been your sister. Same height, same dark hair. Your eyes are even shaped the same."

"What're you leading up to, Susan? That they're finally going to disbar you but I can maybe get a job with Claudia Pfeiffer?"

I told her I was not going to be disbarred and, furthermore, Llewellyn & Llewellyn, even with just one Llewellyn, was not going out of business. Nor would I be cutting her hours or her pay. Not when the firm's future looked so very bright.

"We've got some very important trust work coming up," I said. "And the Office of Lawyer Regulation's inquiry is headed nowhere— for all the scary legal words it threw our way. You know the ones I mean. Misfeasance, embezzlement. And, oh yes, accomplice."

Dawn blinked, then took a long slug of Pepsi before she said, "So what's all this about Claudia Pfeiffer?"

"Claudia's father was my client. Daddy's client, really."

Another operatic sigh, then, "Big construction guy, right? Real estate developer, too."

"Biggest in the city. Julius Augustus Pfeiffer, monarch of all he surveyed, as Daddy put it."

"Doesn't he like own that ugly high-rise they blew up half of East Town to build?"

"Owned," I said. "He died last December."

Dawn's brows drew together. Perhaps she was puzzled as to why none of Julius Pfeiffer's documents had crossed her desk.

I said I'd taken care of his will and all its etceteras personally. "But they're not important. Not when you see what else I found in the Pfeiffer file."

I pulled a piece of paper out of my briefcase and held it up. It read "Certificate of Birth."

Dawn got up from the leather chair, took the paper, then stared at it for a long time. Finally, she said, "Me? Claudia Pfeiffer's daughter?"

She began to grin like she was holding a ticket that hit all five numbers and the PowerBall.

Later, I called Claudia Pfeiffer.

"She bought it," I said.

There was a long pause. Then Claudia laughed. "You're kidding," she said. "Nobody could be that stupid."

"They could be that greedy, though. Dawn already thinks she's the second coming of Princess Di. On the way home tonight, I had to stop her from picking up a brand-new BMW."

"Thank God for greed," Claudia said. "By the way, Susan, please tell me you mean *your* home. And that you didn't leave her alone someplace with her cell phone, proclaiming the good news to everyone she ever knew, along with Channels Four, Twelve, and Fifty-eight."

"Like you said, Claud, nobody could be that stupid. Dawn's asleep in the guest room with half a bottle of Absolut in her."

"I hope that later on she'll be just as easily . . . uh . . . dealt with."

"That, mommy dearest, will be up to you."

"Yes, well," Claudia said. "When do I get to meet my bouncing baby girl?"

"She wanted to drive the Beemer right over. But I said you'd probably need some time to get used to the idea of her."

"Just have the kid on my doorstep soon," Claudia said. "Swaddling clothes optional."

And why was the highborn Claudia Pfeiffer so anxious to claim a proletarian orphan as her own flesh? And would her enthusiasm last once she saw the piercings and the tattoos?

The answers, of course, lay with Julius Augustus Pfeiffer. He wasn't satisfied to build a city. He wanted to found a dynasty.

Unfortunately, his two offspring seemed in no hurry to cooperate. Year after year and marriage after marriage—nothing. He begged them; he threatened them. Until finally three of the best doctors in the state verified what everyone but Julius Augustus already knew. The Pfeiffer twins could not have children.

Furious, uncomprehending, and quite possibly mad, the old man struck back the only way he knew how. He placed all his assets in a trust, then had Daddy draw up a will that stipulated nothing would go to Claudia or her brother until they had children. These children, the will made clear, could be within wedlock or not, just as long as they were Pfeiffers, proven so by law and science. Otherwise, his estate would go to the Society for the Protection of Loons, Divers, and Other Members of Genus Gavia.

Daddy claimed Julius Augustus' mental state was such that the will would never hold up in court. But for once Jack Llewellyn turned out to be wrong and, suddenly, at the age of forty-five, Claudia and Julius II were broke.

Broke, of course, is a relative term. Claudia had some investments of her own, the booty of various divorce settlements. And, after her last divorce, she had moved back into the family house, one of those lavish Lake Drive piles built a hundred years ago by the local robber barons and coveted by every financial upstart since. Julius Pfeiffer had bought it even before he made his first million.

That's where, at lunch one June day, I introduced a grinning Dawn to her mother.

Claudia met the door herself—the poor waif was down to only a yard man and a cleaning woman. We would eat, she said, in the library. As we trailed her through the vast foyer, Dawn's grin grew even broader. The Italian marble floor and pillars clearly impressed her.

"This sure is some place," she whispered. "Like the set of Aida. All it needs is a couple of elephants."

The library held an extensive collection of books, beautifully bound and largely unread, along with portraits of Julius Augustus and Virginia, his consort. There was also one of Julius II. When Claudia saw Dawn staring at the pictures, she said, "My parents and my brother. All of them gone now."

Virginia Pfeiffer had died back in the early nineties and Julius II right after he heard the contents of his father's will. He'd promptly gotten drunk enough to drive his Lamborghini into a highway retaining wall. The car exploded on impact.

Lunch was simple—fresh lake trout, fiddlehead fern salad, some nice wine, and a lot of chatter, mostly between Claudia and me. Dawn kept quiet, from nerves, I suppose. She didn't eat much either, though dessert, Spanische windtorte, was fabulous. Claudia could still afford a good caterer.

After we finished, she suggested Dawn take a peek at the

grounds. "You can go in the boathouse, too, if you wish. It's open."

Dawn, looking both grateful and greedy, bolted for the door.

"Well," I said when she was gone. "What do you think of her?"

"I think you'd better be sure that new birth certificate looks real."

"Of course, it does. Remember all the birth certificates I used to forge in school so we had i.d.? It's the same now as it was then. All you need is the right form, a good pen, and a steady hand."

"You've got chutzpah, I'll say that for you, Susan. And friends in high places."

In low ones, too. Like a clerk in Vital Statistics who saw no harm in letting me work there, nor in leaving me alone to do it. After all, I was an officer of the court—and an old friend of her boss.

Dawn's original birth certificate—the one I replaced with my forgery—listed her mother as Kathleen Anne Siegert. Her father was Unknown. The child's name read Janis Melanie Siegert, the same as on her high school diploma. She'd changed it when she turned eighteen. Had me register her new name with the state, though I told her that wasn't really necessary as long as she didn't use it for purposes of fraud.

Claudia opened a second bottle of wine, filled our glasses, then said, "About the girl's mother—"

"I told you before. No problem."

And there wasn't. Nor would there be.

In the first place, from the moment she'd entered into the adoption agreement, it was as if Dawn's real mother didn't exist. Still, Claudia and I had wanted to be sure the woman would never cause trouble. For all we knew, she might have kept up with Dawn somehow, watched her from afar, and would come swooping down on her newly rich daughter. It didn't seem likely, but the devil really is in the details. I launched a search for Kathleen Siegert.

Once you have someone's Social Security number, she's in your cross hairs; no thicket of married names or criminal aliases can hide her. Kathleen's name had changed only when she married, so it took me but a short while to discover she still lived in the city and owned an import shop in the Third Ward. I also found out she was the widowed mother of two teenage girls. She probably wouldn't be looking for yet a third daughter.

It would've been rather difficult for Kathleen to locate Dawn, anyway, because something had gone wrong at the adoption agency. They couldn't seem to find an appropriate placement. Dawn never knew exactly why, but the upshot was she became one of those "older children" no one seems to want. The agency bounced her into the county welfare system.

By grace or good luck, she turned out to be bright, hardworking, and nobody's fool, a survivor rather than a victim. The kind of young woman anyone would be proud to claim as a daughter.

Claudia agreed. More or less.

"Her grammar's a little iffy and eleven ear studs do verge on excess. She's attractive, though. In a K-Mart kind of way. The tattoos, however, are disappointing."

"That's just her generation."

"I mean they're too small. Too discreet. Though I must admit the Valkyries riding across her back have a certain panache."

"So she'll do?"

"What if I said no?"

I threw up my hands. "Come on, Claud. I've worked on this night and day for the last four months. It hasn't been easy."

"Or cheap," she said. "I've seen your most recent expense account."

"A fake DNA is just a tad expensive."

"You didn't need to pick it up personally. Or fly first class. Or stay almost a week in the most expensive hotel in Boston."

"There were complications," I said.

Which was the understatement of the year. The day before the lab technician was supposed to hand over the report, there'd been an accident at the lab and he'd been killed. It was a shame, of course—the poor man was only thirty-six—to say nothing of inconvenient. The lab took five more days to authorize release of his report.

"At least," Claudia said, "you hadn't paid him off yet."

The woman could be so cheap! I knew I'd have to squeeze her hard to collect my "finder's fee." Good thing her new daughter and I had signed a contract that guaranteed the daughter's personal agent, Susan R. Llewellyn, a very handsome retainer indeed.

That's why I fudged it a bit when Claudia asked for reassurance that Dawn knew nothing about Mr. Pfeiffer's will. "I'd rather not have her appreciate the exact extent to which she has me over the barrel," Claudia said.

Quite truthfully, I said, "She never saw the will. And won't."

When Dawn came back, I left the two of them to get acquainted. I'd done all I could.

Did our plan work? Did Claudia inherit her father's fortune? Did she reward me for my help? The answer to all of the above is: You bet! The DNA test and birth certificate satisfied the terms of Julius Pfeiffer's will, so Claudia began to collect from the trust that held her father's estate. Her monthly allowance was, shall we say, generous. So was my income as sole trustee.

As for Dawn, she got both the BMW and a real mother. To everyone's surprise, she and Claudia bonded almost immediately. It started with their mutual interest in opera, then moved to a genuine emotional attachment. The money helped, of course, but what human relationship is without self-interest? The point is they liked each other and seemed to grow to love each other, too.

They even made up a charming story about how Dawn had begun a search for her birthmother, only to give it up when she discovered who she really was.

"The girl didn't want to come off like some kind of gold-digger," Claudia told her friends. "But then I got wind of it and insisted we meet. Now look at us. Can you believe it?"

Speaking of Dawn's birthmother—in July, Kathleen Kasabian, nee Siegert, was found shot to death in the office of her import shop. The police figured she'd been killed in a late-night robbery—safe was empty and all the security cameras smashed. When I read about it in the Journal Sentinel, I said nothing to Claudia. Why spoil what was happening between her and Dawn?

So far as I could tell, only one fly hovered over the love feast. Well, two flies—the men in their lives. Claudia had a new fiancé and Dawn was seeing her old boyfriend, Mike.

Though Claudia privately called Mike a creep she wished had stayed in the Marines, she let me talk her into giving him work at one of the Pfeiffer companies.

"He can be . . . uh . . . dealt with later," I said.

For her part, Dawn never said much about Claudia's fiancé. But I could tell she didn't care for him. Nor did I, for the simple reason that Nelson Schwann was far too interested in the Pfeiffer Trust. He began sniffing around almost from the moment he loaded the four carets onto Claudia's finger.

As Trustee, I headed him off as long as I could. But the president of one of the city's largest banks is a hard man to play games with. Finally, I told Claudia that if she wanted Nelson to go over the books, I was ready for him.

A few evenings later, Claudia and Nelson appeared in my office. It was well after business hours and at a time when no one else was in the building. He carried a large briefcase loaded, I assumed, with the heavy artillery of an audit. Claudia had a tartan-topped picnic basket in her hand. "I brought supper," she said. "Just sandwiches and some white wine."

I managed a smile as I took the basket and set it on my new secretary's desk—Dawn had apparently decided her time was now better spent in the opera houses of Europe. I kept smiling as we went into my office.

Nelson, a tall blond man, was groomed and tailored to look ten years younger and fifteen pounds lighter than he really was. Even so, he still came across as middle aged. I suspected he always had.

They sat in the leather chairs, Nelson's briefcase on the oriental rug between them, and I took my place behind the desk—to gaze across its cluttered expanse at my guests and the door to the outer office. Closed now, it still bore a poster touting last year's production of La Cenerentala.

When we were settled, Nelson said, "I hear you're a woman of many talents."

"What's that supposed to mean?"

"It's what your ex-husband tells me. We play handball together at the Athletic Club, He also says you're a very gutsy lady."

"I can't believe he'd be so kind."

"Well, he does claim you have the moral sensibility of a wolverine."

After I finished laughing, Nelson said, "Only this time you've gone after prey far too large."

He reached in his briefcase to bring out a thick sheaf of computer printouts. They proved, he said, just how, and to what extent, I had gutted the Pfeiffer Trust.

As I stared at the printouts, Claudia said, "I must admit, Susan, I was very impressed with what you did to the Trust."

She ran a hand through her salt and pepper hair. "Almost as

impressed as I was with what you did to my brother."

Now I stared at Claudia.

She said, "Your ex was right about your talents. Master forger, creative accountant. And demolition expert. The bomb in my brother's car was clever. All he had to do was sideswipe something, anything, and kahboom."

I went cold, then hot, then cold again. "The police never—"

"That lab technician's death was well handled, too. At first I wondered how you pulled it off without blowing up the lab and everyone in it."

She reached over and touched Nelson's hand. "But Nelson tells me that in the workplace, even after 9/11, people will still open any package with their name on it. He says one could send an ICBM. And, of course, a competent bomb-maker can more or less limit the explosion."

My throat felt like there was a rock in it. I couldn't speak. I could hardly even breathe.

Claudia said, "You were so resourceful with the bombs, I wonder why you changed your—what do they call it on television?— your M.O. Why did you shoot Dawn's birthmother?"

I was still unable to speak when she leaned across my desk and began to fiddle with the intercom.

Nelson said, "Is it working?"

"Yes," Claudia said. "Recording every word."

That's when I finally found my voice. "What is this, Claud?"

"Why, it's your confession."

I slapped the intercom—to turn it off, break it, whatever.

"Don't bother," Nelson said. "The whole office is bugged. Telephone, lamps, computer. Real James Bond stuff."

I couldn't believe it. "Do you honestly think I'm going to confess to killing all those people?"

"Even if you don't," Claudia said, "I think we've got enough evidence to take to the police."

"Evidence of embezzlement, too," Nelson added, patting the printouts.

I said I didn't know anything about bombs. "So how could I possibly blow anybody up?"

Then something occurred to me. "You're the one who'd know about explosives, Claud. Your father's whole career was based on blowing up old buildings. Pfeiffer Demolition made him his first million."

Nelson stood up and went to one of the bookcases. He touched a volume. "Well, well," he said. "A book on making bombs."

He waved at the shelf it sat on. "And here's half a dozen more."

Claudia said, "You've a similar collection at home. Which you should have destroyed, by the way. Then there's all that information on bombs you downloaded from the Internet."

I glanced from her to Nelson. How rich and sleek they looked, he in his bespoke suit, she in her handmade shoes. And how smug.

"Now I get it," I said. "I'm supposed to be the fall guy in all this."

"Hardly."

"I think I even know how you pulled it off, Claud. When your father died, you got rid of the co-heir immediately. No trick, that. It wasn't the first time your alcoholic brother'd cracked up a car. Then you did the guy at the lab—Kathleen Kasabian, too—so nobody'd ever claim Dawn's not your daughter."

Claudia shook her head.

"And you want me to take the rap," I said. "I can understand that. What I don't understand is why you don't just blow me away like the others."

Nelson's eyes went to his briefcase. Was there a bomb in it? Or in that picnic basket in the outer office?

Now I was scared. I had to get out of there.

But Nelson was a big man. He could stop me before I even made it up from my chair. And I'd sure need more help than my clever tongue could deliver. I'd need the .38 in my desk drawer.

Hands shaking, I slipped the drawer key from its hiding place under the computer, palmed it, then somehow stuck it in the lock. All this, I made sure, without being seen.

Meanwhile, I said, "I might've cooked the Trust's books, but—"

"So you admit it?" Nelson said.

I yanked open the desk drawer and grabbed for the gun.

It wasn't there.

The office door swung open then and in came Dawn. She held the picnic basket in one hand, my snub nose .38 in the other.

Turning toward her, Claudia said, "Did you hear all that?"

"Over the intercom?" Dawn said. "Sure. But she didn't confess to much."

"She will," Nelson said. "When that gun's to her head."

Revolver still pointed my way, Dawn came over and set the basket on a corner of the desk.

"You better look at this," she said as she pulled back the basket's tartan lid.

Somehow I managed to stand up and peer inside. Except in the movies, I'd never seen a pipe bomb. But a length of capped pipe wired to a clock and a 9-volt battery gives you the clue. I knew it for what it was.

I pulled my eyes away from the bomb just as Dawn turned to Nelson. "You're a greedy pig," she said. "You want my inheritance."

Then she shot him dead.

As he fell next to the bookcase, she shot Claudia, too.

For a while, we both watched Claudia's body slide off the leather chair onto the oriental rug. Silence and the smell of cordite filled the room.

Later, in my Range Rover with me at the wheel and Strauss's Elektra on the CD player, Dawn said, "Good thing you never registered the .38. We could of been in deep shit after Kathleen."

As we left the parking ramp and turned onto Wisconsin Avenue, I asked where we were headed.

"Over to Mike's. I am, anyways. But first pull in that alley."

When we parked, she turned off the music but kept the dashboard cloak on. "It won't be long now," she said. "Beforehand, though, I wanna tell you that you were right about Claudia sending the bomb to the lab tech. And how come my real mom got killed."

In the glow of the clock, Dawn looked as green as I felt.

"Claud's brother?" she said. "Who knows. Maybe she did it, maybe he was drunk just like the cops thought."

She pulled the picnic basket out of the foot well and held it on her lap. "Mike put this together," she said. "The bomb, I mean. I put it in the basket. There's another one in a file cabinet back at your office."

Mike, she told me, had learned all about explosives at Pfeiffer Demolition. "So aren't you glad you got him the job?"

I still said nothing, and we sat in silence until we heard the explosion in my office.

Dawn let out a loud "Yes!" Then she put the basket back in the foot well.

"I'm kinda sorry about this, Susan," she said. "You were always like a mom to me. Taught me a lot, too. But in fifteen minutes—well, it's gonna look like you made a fatal mistake."

As Dawn climbed out of the vehicle, the thought of my being a mother to her must have lingered in her mind. Or maybe it was Claudia she recalled. Whichever, she paused a moment and, turning back to me, said, "If this was an opera, right now everybody'd be going, 'Addio, mia madre, addio, addio, addio.' "

That was twelve minutes ago. I'm still in the Range Rover, nylon handcuffs still binding my hands to the steering wheel.

Yeah. Addio.

The End

Winner of *Futures Mysterious Anthology Magazine* Slesar's Twist Contest.

TEN LITTLE GANGSTERS

Me and Big Al were by ourselves in his Wisconsin place that fall morning, the rest of the boys being asleep in their tents or up the guard towers. I was practicing bank shots on the green-cloth in the parlor. Al was upstairs with a little blonde from Hayward.

So everything stood still and peaceable when Charley the Finn came skidding up the lane in that whiney flivver of his. Out he flopped, yowling for Al to come rescue him.

"Snorky," he yelled, calling Al by the nickname nobody ever said he could use. "Snorky, sumpin's gone wrong over at Short Nap's."

I ran outside and waved off the two boys charging up the lane, tommies at the ready. "'S OK," I hollered at them. "He's a pal."

"Snorky," Charley yelled again.

I grabbed him by his canvas galluses. "He's Mr. Capone to you and quit your yipping at him."

"It's terrible over there, Bill."

"That's Mr. Dekydd to you."

"Gimme a break, will ya," Charley said, still all aflutter. "Everybody over there got it."

I had nary an idea what he meant 'cause you can't hardly understand those Up North yokels. They talk like they got mashed turnip stuck on their tonsils. I was about to shut him up but good when Al stuck his head out an upstairs window. "What's going on down there?"

"They're pfft, Snorky. All of 'em," Charley told him. "And I don't know how they got that way."

Me, I'd of thrown the dumb s.o.b. back in the tamarack swamp he crawled out of. But Al's a Christian. He said, "Come on in the house, Charley. Then you can tell me about it."

91

On the way inside, Charley fell to blubbering even harder. "Short Nap's dead. They all are."

Short Nap was Napoleon Short and I didn't care if the fat little bootlegger had knocked back his last finger of skee. Al sure wouldn't, either. Looked like the only one did was Charley the Finn.

But what did he mean, everybody'd got huffed?

When Charley was in the living room warming his cheeks by the fire, Al came downstairs. He looked snorky as ever, all dressed up in his new hunting duds—leather jerkin, buffalo-plaid shirt, tweed britches tucked in high-top gum boots. He had a khaki hunting coat slung over his arm and a Jones cap in his hand.

It was pretty much the same outfit I had on. Everybody else, too. That's what I liked about Al, he wanted his boys turned out good as him even when he had to pay Marshall Fields $125 a man to get it done.

Not that me and Al looked alike. We were about the same age—I turned twenty-eight that year—but he was a lot bigger, only a couple inches under six foot and heavy along with it. I was still skinny then, with a thick thatch of ginger hair and blue peeps I didn't need specs to see out.

Charley? He just looked like hell.

"Get the man a drink," Al said. "And not any of that backwoods hooch they make up here. Stuff'll kill you. Give him some of the real thing from Chicago."

What I wanted to give Charley was a kick in his britches. Boy had no business bothering Al on a Sunday morning. But I did like I was told and pulled a pony of needle beer out of the icebox. Chicago-made all right, but just near beer with a little alcohol shot in. I was blamed if I'd waste a bottle of South Side brew on the likes of squonking Charley in there.

Me, I'm Al's pick triggerman. Name's Bill Dekydd. Well, John Wilkes Dekydd, if you want to get legal about it. But I'm from down Arkansas way and when I first came up here, folks just had to call me Arky. A couple busted snoots later and they agreed on Bill. Which is what my daddy wanted to name me in the first place, but Mama, who's not over the War yet, held out for John Wilkes.

Back in the parlor, Al had listened to Charley's story. When I came in with the beer, he was grinning at Charley. "Don't let the trouble over at Nap's keep you on the anxious seat," he said. "I'll get it simplized for you."

Good as that might've sounded, Charley was still sweating bullets. Didn't blame him. You never knew with Al. He could be all glad-eye one second and killing crazy the next. I remember once in a blind pig in Cicero he was yucking it up with some Chicago bulls when one of 'em went and called him Scarface. Fellow was probably just dumb and drunk, but it still wasn't a healthy thing for even a cop to say. Five minutes later, he came to with his beezer in the sawdust, a roscoe to his conk, and the Big Fellow on his back. Then he went for a little ride.

On t'other hand, Al liked to help folks, "Public service is my motto,"* he always said. It was Al that set the law on those two college punks killed that little boy back in '24 and he always got the Pinkertons off after they busted up a union man. He'd travel all over the country, too, go wherever a pal was in trouble—New York, Miami, Colorado, Los Angeles. Lordy, the man even went to Iowa.

That's pretty much how I got on with the Big Fellow. When he came down to Hot Springs in '25 to help my boss close up a mitt joint, he took a liking to the way I could fire a shotgun out of either fist, separate or together. "If you're ever in Chi," he said, "look me up. I'll find you a job."

A week later I was headed for Yankeeland.

Now, in the parlor of his hunting cabin, Al clapped Charley on the back. "At least Nap's out of the way. As for the rest of it . . ."

He turned to me. "We're going over to Nap's. You, me, and Charley here. Get somebody good to drive. What you packing, Charley?"

Charley tapped his jacket. "Belly gun," he said.

Al jerked his thumb at the gun case over by the stairs. "Take the sawyers, Bill, and a couple choppers."

Jumping Jerusalem, I thought. Tommy guns and sawed-offs both. What's he expecting to find at Short Nap's cabin?

That's what the driver wondered, too, when he came up to the house. "Big trouble, huh?" he said. "I'll take da goil back to town."

"Nope," I said. "Somebody else'll carry her back."

His name was Edward G. Caesar and he thought he was the sheik of Araby, sporting those long, pointy sideburns and black hair he currycombed with Wildroot. Truth be known, Eddy was just a dem, dese, dose guy out of Brooklyn. And he was even harder to understand than Charley. Al should've made him go to night school, like he did me. "You want to be somebody," Al always said, "you gotta sound like a gent."

Eddy said—leastways I think he said, "We better stick da heat under da floor board. Don't want some backwoods deputy getting put to bed 'cause he seen what he shouldn't."

"Laws is way too dainty, come out on a day like this," I said.

A storm'd begun in the night, a rip snorter with hard rain and big wind. By now, late morning, only the rain kept on. Sometimes it was just cold spit, then it'd up and turn to a real goose-drownder.

"Dem roads gonna be bad," Eddy said. "Maybe Mr. Capone oughtta go a different day."

You ask me, Eddy didn't want to go. The boy could drive better than Barney Olds himself, but that's all she wrote. He was a one-trick pony. When the lead started flying, Eddy headed for the can.

We took one of the closed cars, an A sedan, maybe not the flashiest car in the fleet, but the weather was too cold for a flivver and the muddy roads couldn't handle Al's big, lead-lined Caddy.

Usually, Eddy drove, with me riding shotgun and Al tucked safe and sound behind us. Today, though, Al said he'd get up front with Eddy and I should sit with Charley in the back.

"Rats!" I said and hauled out my pocket pistol, took a swig, then offered it to Eddy.

"Stuff come with you from Chicago? 'Cause I ain't drinking no rot-gut from up here. No telling what dese dumb rubes put in it."

"This here's genuine Cutty Sark Scotch," I told him. "Straight off one of Mr. Joe Kennedy's own boats."

Eddy took the flask. When he handed it back, it was plumb empty.

Fact is, Eddy needed every drop of whiskey he could drink. We all did. The trip to Short Nap's place turned out to be thirty miles of pure woe. That country up there's either hill or swamp. And back then, the North Woods being pretty much lumbered out, it was covered with nothing but bramble bush, mossy old stumps, and straggly young pine. The roads? Even the ones with highway numbers weren't much more than jumped-up logging tracks.

And that was on the best of days. This day, the rain'd turned them into hog wallows. For three long hours we either rode in water lapping at the running boards or bumped up and down one rocky grade after another. I can't recollect how many times we had to get out and push. Al, too, huffing and puffing and cussing in two lingoes.

Worse yet, when we weren't stuck in the mud, I was stuck listening to Charley Dumdum from Duluth explain how he came to be so powerful interested in Napoleon Short from Chi-town.

The cause was about what you'd expect—Short Nap tried to horn in on Charley's rum fleet. The year before, somebody put a couple new sneakers on Superior to carry the groceries out of Canada. At first, Charley ignored it. He had plenty putt-putts of his own, never mind aeroplanes moving pig iron summer and winter both. Then the Mounties made a couple seizures and you didn't have to be bit by a fox to figure out who paid them for their trouble.

"So," Charley said, "I decided I better take Nap out. Do it during duck season. Make it look like he got tangled up in his 12-gauge."

Charley figured his plan would work because Al wasn't the only Chicago businessman that took vacations in northern Wisconsin. Over to Barker Lake a Joliet boy was building himself a golf course and Al's own brother had land near Mercer. But Short Nap had gone and done everybody one better. He bought a whole island.

It stood in a big lake called Sis-koom-bah or some such and lay so deep in the middle of nowhere even the Chippewa'd never heard of it. Besides that, Charley told us, after you finally found the old lumber track that served for Nap's lane and wound around for a bunch of miles, all you came to was the bank of the lake. And that was nothing but lily pads and fallen logs and big patches of wild rice.

"If Nap expects you," Charley said, "you find a boat. And the dingdang lake's so big, even if you light down in a sea gull, you still need a boat."

'Course, Nap had guards posted at his boat launch. Charley said they stayed in an old Army tent with nothing much to do but play cards and gripe about their miseries. Couldn't blame 'em. It's no fun sleeping on a spindly cot with the coon prowling round and the deer mice eating your smokes.

When we pulled up to the guard post, we didn't find any mice or coon or cards. Nap's guards, neither. What we found was two stiffs and Ross Kolnikov.

Ross was the boy Charley planned to turn loose on Short Nap once he had him trapped on his island. Instead, all poor Ross got to do was shiver in the damp while Charley ran for Al.

"Anything new?" Charley asked him when he met the car.

Ross blinked at him. "Never seen nothing."

Matter of fact, there wasn't much to see. Just the guards' tent and a couple of boats tied up to the rickety little pier.

Al looked pretty disgusted about this arrangement and I expect he was. Al never went after anything or anybody without a solid angle and lots of backup.

Charley explained how he'd planned a night raid on Nap by canoe, the one at the pier. But about midnight when he and Ross snuck up to the tent, ready to blow the guards to their Maker, they found them stone dead in a wallow of guns and bottles and puddles of puke.

Now Nap's triggermen lay in the tent under a piece of tarp. When Eddy peeled it back, Al gazed down on the two boys and shook his head. "We're making a shooting gallery out of a great business," he said. "And nobody is profiting."*

But they hadn't been shot. Nor hooked or dug. Strangled, neither.

However they got dead, I recognized one of them as Jack di Rippa, an old boy the newspapers liked to describe as "a known criminal, with a special fondness for aging street walkers."

Charley poked a toe toward the t'other, a dark little fellow with a wine bottle by his hand. "Used to be one of my mugs," he said. "Name of Shicklgruber. Just off the boat and always bragging about some cousin back in the old country—politician, paperhanger, something like that."

By now Al was mad, like he always got when good Joes clicked it. "I curse whoever done this," he shouted, shaking his cigar in the air.

His face turned dark red and his scars started to glow like white-hot coals. "Why can't we treat our business like any other man treats his, something to work at in the daytime and forget when he goes home at night? There's plenty of business for everybody. Why kill each other over it?"*

Then Al was all at once calm again. "OK, Charley," he said. "Let's get back to your plan for Nap. How'd you keep tabs on him?"

"Just had him followed around," Charley said. "He never seemed to care, even bought the trailer a Green River one time.

Anybody got a fag?"

Eddy broke out a pack of humps and both men lit up.

Charley said, "I had the island staked out all summer and fall—fellows on the lake looking like fishermen or in the brush making like poachers. Even got some Chippewa to keep an eye on the place while they was gathering the wild rice."

"Nap come out to the island a lot?"

"Not once since June. Nobody else, neither. Even the guards never went over 'cause there wasn't a boat for 'em to use. Nap brought the only one with him yesterday."

Charley pointed his Camel toward the big rowboat by the pier. "Him and the others came in the afternoon and the Kraut rowed 'em out to the island. Took a couple trips."

I said, "How you know that?"

"He already told ya," Eddy said, jerking his butt right up to my kisser. "Charley was on their tail and even a hillbilly like you musta hoid of field glasses."

This was going to be the end of Edward G. Caesar. "Listen, you yeller Yankee—"

Big Al stepped in. "Cut it out, both of you. Think about these two dead fellows. What do you want to do, get yourself killed before you're thirty? You'd better get some sense while a few of us are left alive."*

While Charley rowed Al and me and Eddy across the lake—Ross stayed with the stiffs—I could see the island was as naked as the rest of that poor, timbered-out country. Except for a blanket of bush and a little stand of cedar, the island was picked clean as a chicken at Christmas.

Which was just the way Nap planned it. "Nobody's gonna jump outta the woods at me," he once told Al. "And with the lake for protection, I don't have to bother building guard towers."

As for his big log house, it sure wasn't the kind of cabin I grew up in—ramshackle pine over the dirt floor swarming with young'uns and a pack of hounds to keep you from freezing to death come January. No siree, this house was made of fat brown logs with a shake roof and pretty green shutters that would've looked good even in Winnetka.

After we tied up at the island pier, Al told Eddy to check out the three little outbuildings, then come back and stay with the boat.

"We're going in the house," he said to me and Charley. "Get out your gat, Charley. Bill, you bring our guns."

The rain started in again as we walked up the gravel path, Al smoking his cigar, me carrying the bag of iron, Charley pointing a .38 at his foot.

The big oak front door, with irises and what looked like a beehive carved into it, stood wide open. Al sent Charley inside to see if the place was like he'd left it.

"Just like it," Charley said when he came back, though he didn't look happy over saying so.

Al and me stepped into what Short Nap likely called his foyer but which looked more like the hat check at the Aragon Ballroom. It held fur coats and fedoras, cloaks and cloches. A brown deerstalker hung from a wooden peg.

"Uh-oh," Al said when he saw the dead guy on the wide-planked floor.

"Just like when I was here before," Charley said.

Al stooped to look at the body. "Willy the Shake Iago," he said. "Ex-doughboy, like all Nap's triggermen. Heard he won lots of medals in the war. Much good they did him in here."

Next to Willy was a silver hip hootch. A Chicago typewriter leaned against the wall.

We stepped over Iago's body and into the dining room.

"Will you look at this," Al said when he saw the room. "Place is bigger than Holy Name Cathedral."

It was something all right, with a bank of windows running along one whole side, walk-in fireplaces at each end, and log rafters big around as Al's waist. Wide flagstone hearths held half a dozen overstuffed chairs made out of purple plush with little gold irises woven in. Above the fireplaces—their fires still a-smolder—hung the prettiest stuffed heads you ever did see.

Stretched twixt the two fireplaces was a long table covered with a fancy white cloth. On it sat liquor bottles and silver forks and china eatware. It also bore the remains of a fat Virginia ham and three dead men.

Not just any dead men, either. Slumped on that table were the corpses of some of the best bootleggers in Senator Volstead's America.

We gazed at them, real quiet-like, till Al broke in. "Now ain't this just a shame?" he said.

Then he smiled.

"Whatcha think happened here, Mister Capone?" Charley asked.

"You tell us, bright boy."

"I . . . I . . . I . . ."

"Ah, shut up and lemme think," Al said.

The room was just like the guard tent—a little puke and no blood at all. Short Nap, decked out in a come-to-Jesus suit, sat slumped in his chair at the head of the table. On his left, half fallen on the floor, was a young fellow also wearing tails.

"Mickey Carleone," Al said with a sigh. "From back east. I do business with his brother Don. He's gonna be awful sore about this."

Further along the table came still another man in a monkey suit—Dr. Arthur C. Moriarity, face smack down in his plate. Doc used to teach chemistry at some jerkwater college out in Iowa. That is, till Big Al came to town and learned him real chemistry.

"Look at all that booze, will ya," Charley said, pointing at the table.

And he was right. There was bottle on bottle. I don't know how many or what they all held. Lots of whiskey, for sure, every bottle of it with a label claiming it was genuine bottled-in-the-bond. No siree, no aged-in-the-barn squirrel dew on Napoleon Short's table. Just plenty of old French cream, lots of Minnehaha water, and veeno in every color of the rainbow.

I'd set the guns down and picked up a bottle of something called amaretto—it smelled like nuts—when I noticed that a few of the embroidered chairs around the table stood empty. While Al and Charley were still tut-tutting, I pulled up the table cloth.

"There's three skirts under here," I said.

Al's eyes slewed toward Charley. "Didn't you say you only saw two get in the boat?"

"I thought I seen just the two, but how do you know these days? The broads all got their hairs bobbed."

"Well, there's three here now," I said. "And one deader'n the next."

"Haul 'em out," Al said. "So we can get 'em sorted."

Charlie and I grabbed a pair of silk-stockinged mumblypegs and yanked. Out from under the table came the body of a black-headed jane. She was maybe twenty years old and dressed fit to kill in a green evening frock.

When Al saw her, he nodded his head. "Shouldn't be a surprise," he said.

I asked how come.

"Know who this frail is? This is Antonia Metz-Soprano," Al said. "From back east."

Back east folks were always erasing each other.

"The Metz-Sopranos have been singing," Al said.

"To John Law?"

"The Feds."

"Can they carry a tune?" I asked.

"Depends on whose listening."

I said, "If it's another'n like that Elliott Mess, no point getting all lathered-up. Boy smashes a couple beer barrels, thinks he oughtta have a Congressional Medal. Fact is, him and them gumps of his couldn't find their way outta the Loop without calling in the Rainbow Girls."

Al grinned. "There's a lot of mob guys might not be casual as you where it comes to squawkers."

He took out his Cuban stogies, offered them around. "How about it, Charley?"

Charley nearly had his cigar lit before he figured out what Al was getting at.

"Jeepers, Mr. Capone," he said, the havana dropping from his fingers. "I didn't do this. I swear on my grandmother's knees I didn't."

Al grinned again. "I know you didn't. Whoever did's got more than cheese for brains."

Charley couldn't dare take offense, so he picked up the cigar and went to stand by the window, smoking and peering into the drizzle.

Me, I'd passed on the stogy—I'd rather blow up a tailor-made Fatima—and was taking a looksee at the Metz-Soprano dame. "No blood on her. Only a little puke, just like on the men."

When we pulled out the other two bodies—a redhead and a blonde, both bottle jobs—it was the same.

"How many's that make now?" Al asked.

I ticked them off on my fingers—the three triggermen, the six at the dinner table. "Nine," I said.

Al again shook his head in puzzlement.

After a while he said, "Know who the two fems are, don't you?"

"Sure. Bessy James and that doll Doc Moriarity's been playing with lately."

"Bessy was Short Nap's payoff man, you know. Very smart lady."

"If she was so smart," I said, "how'd she wind up under a dinner table, dead as any Dumb Dora?"

From his spot by the window, Charley said, "Never seen how he could put a frill in charge of his brass."

Al said, "Nap stumbled onto her when she was just a kid in his stable. She wasn't much good on the game, he claimed. But, oh boy, could she diddle numbers."

Al squatted beside red-haired Bessy, his britches stretched almost as tight over his wide butt as the black silk crepe was over hers. He lifted her diamond choker to show a yellow iris tattoo.

"Nap always liked a union label on his merchandise," I said.

"Bet we won't find any tattoos on that one," Al said, nodding at the other gal. "Her name's Annabelle Lecter and she's a student dietitian."

Annabelle, blond as Mary Pickford, had on a white middy blouse, pleated tweed skirt, kid-leather oxfords.

"Girl must've got the wrong invitation," Al said as he stood up. "She sure isn't dressed for a formal supfest like everybody else is."

"But she's cold meat anyhow," Charley said.

"Out," Al told him, cocking a thumb toward the door. "Now."

When Charley had gone, Al picked up one of the wine bottles. It was labeled Chateau de Froggy or some such, though I doubted anything French was inside. Short Nap had a cellar full of fancy labels, and the fakers to print them.

Al sniffed at the wine bottle and a couple of other empties. Then he held some of the gin and whiskey bottles to the light before opening and sniffing them, too.

"Did Charley say who brought the liquor?" he asked.

"Said Nap brought it all up hisself, early in the summer. Said Nap's boys wouldn't let anybody else come on the island with so much as a split in their hand."

Al already knew—and it was a sore point with him—that Nap would only drink, or serve, his own stuff. Even when he sat in Al's offices at the Hawthorne Hotel, smoking Al's Cubans, he still sipped from the tickler he kept in his pocket.

"Look for his flask," Al told me. "The others', too. Bessy'll have hers strapped to her right thigh."

I grinned when I found it. Al was some hijacker all right.

Meantime, he'd set to inspecting the Virginia ham and its fixings, poking and slicing and sniffing. But never, I saw, tasting of anything.

When he was done with the table and the flasks, he went to the kitchen. Except for the boxes the food came in—they were from a North Avenue delicatessen—the kitchen was cold, damp, and empty.

Back in the dining room, Al ran a hand over the whiskers he liked to raise when he came Up North. He still looked puzzled.

He was poking around in the ash trays on the table and I'd moseyed over to the windows when Charley came bursting back in. "Al, come quick! Eddy's pooped."

Sure enough, inside one of Short Nap's sheds, Eddy lay dead. I can't say I was very sorry about it.

There was no blood on the shed's dirt floor or on any of the rough, empty shelves and when Charley checked Eddy over, all he found was a pearl-handled .44, a half-empty wine split, and two herds of Camels.

Al asked Charley what was in the other two sheds.

"One of 'em's empty," Charley said. "The other's just got a bunch of dead soldiers in it."

Back in the house, we stood by one of the big fireplaces, smoking and warming up. Al went back to scratching his whiskers.

Presently, Charley got glasses and an unopened bottle of wine from the table. When he'd found a corkscrew, he pulled the plug and poured three goodly dollops of some French stuff.

As Al and me stuck our noses in our glasses, Charley raised his and uttered every bootlegger's favorite toast—"Prohibition now, Prohibition tomorrow, Prohibition forever."

The words were barely in the air when Al's glass went splintering onto the stone hearth. He slapped away my own glass, then Charley's.

While me and Charley stood there with our jaws around our belt buckles, Al pointed at the broken glass and spilt wine. "Poison," he said.

"Hunh?"

"You dopes!" Al said. "They've all been poisoned. The ones in here, that boy in the hall, Eddy, the ones across the lake. All of 'em."

He wheeled on Charley. "And I don't like it! Poison just ain't American! My rackets are run on strictly American lines and they're going to stay that way."*

For a minute, Charley looked like he'd been smacked with an oak towel.

I said, "What you mean, poison?"

"Can't you smell it?"

"Hunh?"

"The bitter almond," Al said. "It's cyanide."

I'd smelled something like almonds around the table, but I thought it came from that amaretto stuff. Charley, finding himself still among the living, swore he didn't smell a thing.

We went to the table, where Al picked up one of the wine bottles and shoved it under my nose. "Smell it?"

I did. "But how you know it's cyanide?"

"Read about it in Agatha Christie," Al said, and right then I decided I better get my own set of the Harvard Classics.

"I never poisoned nobody," Charley said. He was still plenty scared.

Lucky for Charley, Al had calmed down. "I know you didn't," he said. "And I'll prove it. Go out to that shed and bring back half a dozen dead soldiers."

When Charley'd gone, I said, "If Charley didn't kill 'em, who did?"

Al settled his bulk in one of the purple plush easy chairs. Folding diamond-ringed hands over his belly, he said, "It was an accident."

I picked up on the notion right off. "So you're saying Nap wanted to do Doc or the Carleone kid and slipped up, put poison in everybody's drinks."

"Now, now, Bill," the Big Fellow said. "You know Nap was too smart for that."

I pointed at the table. "One of them did it, then."

"They couldn't of delivered enough poison."

"Not even Doc or his dietitian gal?"

"Use your head, Bill. Think Nap's boys woulda taken a drink off Doc Moriarity, much less his girlfriend?"

"That brings us back to Charley."

"Charley's a man!" Al snapped. "He'da come in with guns blazing."

Charley came in now, arms loaded with empty wine bottles.

"Take a whiff of 'em," Al said.

Sure enough, the bottles smelt of bitter almonds.

Al said, "You boys know plenty about making hooch. But you don't know anything about wine, do you?"

We admitted we didn't.

"When you make wine, 'specially white wine, and you want it to look and taste real good, you have to do something to clarify it," he said. "That's called fining and most often it's done with cyanide."

Al lit a havana. "I won't bore you with all of how it works, but sometimes it doesn't go right and the wine gets poisoned."

"You didn't learn that out of no book," I said. "More like in your daddy's basement."

Al winked at me and puffed his stogy.

But I was still a little confused. "How come these folks went and downed what was pretty much straight prussic acid?"

"Simple," Al said. "Nap's booze is always so bad, nobody knew what they were drinking."

"We're sure in a tough business," I said.

"You're right about that," Al said, sounding a mite sad. "It's a thankless one and full of grief."*

By now, Charley had stuck his nose in half a dozen wine bottles. Finally, looking like a Bluetick that can't tree his coon, he turned to Al. "Don't smell like nothing," he said.

"These stiffs sure will pretty soon," Al said, standing up. "Let's go, Bill."

Charley let out a yelp. "But, Mr. Capone, that's why I come to you. I don't know what I'm s'posed to do with all these dead people. The cops'll think I killed 'em."

"What were you gonna do after you and Ross came in here with your artillery?"

"Roll 'em in the lake?" Charley said, not sounding too sure about it.

"Well, do what you have to. And don't worry about the cops. I'll get the blame anyhow. They've already hung everything on me but the Chicago fire."*

A few days later, as we drove back to Chicago, Al said, "You know, boys, you gotta have a product that everybody needs every day. We don't have it in booze. Except for the lushes, most people only buy a couple of fifths of gin or Scotch when they're having a party. The workingman laps up half a dozen bottles of beer on Saturday night, and that's it for the week."

It had quit raining and afternoon sun now poured over the Wisconsin countryside.

"But with milk!" Al said. "Every family wants it on the table. The people on Lake Shore Drive want thick cream in their coffee. The big families out back of the yards have to buy a couple of gallons of fresh milk every day for the kids . . . Do you guys know there's a bigger markup in fresh milk than there is in alcohol? Honest to God, we've been in the wrong racket right along."*

The End

* Alphonse Capone, quoted in Mark Levell and Bill Helmer, eds. *The Quotable Al Capone* (Chicago and Crestwood, IL: The Chicago Typewriter Co. & Mad Dog Press, 1990).

ABOUT THE AUTHOR

MJ Jones grew up in Wisconsin and lives there now. She taught college English in the South and Midwest. Her crime fiction has appeared in Alfred Hitchcock's Mystery Magazine, Scribblers & Ink Spillers, and elsewhere in print and online. Her story "The Witch and the Relic Thief" received Mystery Writers of America's Robert L. Fish Memorial Award for Best First Short Story.

www.MJJonesMysteries.com

www.ingramcontent.com/pod-product-compliance
Lightning Source LLC
Chambersburg PA
CBHW030639130626
46552CB00002B/932